“Looks like our little girl has had enough for today.”

Our little girl. Was that how he thought of them—as a family?

“She’s so beautiful when she’s asleep.”

“And quiet.”

Tori nodded. “She does like to talk.” Softly they made their way back downstairs.

He gazed her way and smiled. Her breath caught. His smile stole the starch from her knees. It was wide and warm and utterly charming. There was a small crease on one side of his mouth that was completely adorable. She couldn’t look away.

“Is everything all right?”

She nodded. “You should do that more often.”

“What?”

“Smile.”

He drew his finger across his chin as if embarrassed. “I haven’t had much to smile about in the last few years.”

“Well, it’s quite a sight.”

“You think so?”

“I do.”

“Then, I’ll try to find more reasons to display it.”

Tori looked into his eyes and saw a warmth and lightness she’d never seen before.

Lorraine Beatty was raised in Columbus, Ohio, but now calls Mississippi home. She and her husband, Joe, have two sons and five grandchildren. Lorraine started writing in junior high and is a member of RWA and ACFW, and is a charter member and past president of Magnolia State Romance Writers. In her spare time she likes to work in her garden, travel and spend time with her family.

Books by Lorraine Beatty

Love Inspired

Home to Dover

Protecting the Widow's Heart
His Small-Town Family
Bachelor to the Rescue
Her Christmas Hero
The Nanny's Secret Child
A Mom for Christmas
The Lawman's Secret Son
Her Handyman Hero

Rekindled Romance
Restoring His Heart

Her Handyman Hero

Lorraine Beatty

Recycling programs for this product may not exist in your area.

ISBN-13: 978-1-335-42784-7

Her Handyman Hero

This edition published by arrangement with Love Inspired Books.

www.Harlequin.com

Printed in U.S.A.

But thou, O Lord, art a God full of compassion,
and gracious, long suffering,
and plenteous in mercy and truth.

—*Psalms* 86:15

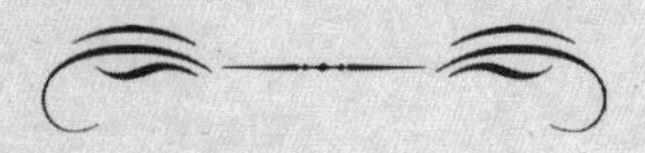

To my husband, Joe, for being my real-life hero.
Your help and support mean more
than you'll ever know. I love you.

Chapter One

The house looked like a riverboat that had been dropped into the middle of a lush green yard.

Reid Blackthorn frowned, puzzling over what he was seeing. The old white Victorian was ringed on two levels with wraparound porches dripping with gingerbread and ornately turned posts and spindles. The stately tower perched on top of the roof resembled a steamboat wheelhouse. All it lacked was a large red paddle wheel to complete the picture. It wasn't what he had expected to find when he came looking for the woman who had taken his niece.

He rubbed his forehead and inhaled a calming breath. Legally, Victoria Montgomery was his niece's guardian, but he was prepared to change that if possible. His last disastrous undercover assignment for the DEA had made him realize he wanted more than chasing drug dealers. He was empty and burned-out. All he wanted now was a quiet, peaceful existence. His first move had been tracking down his younger brother in hopes of making amends for not honoring their mother's dying wish. Reid had promised to take care of Eddie, but instead Reid had followed his need for justice and never looked back.

He'd found Eddie in a hospital dying from years of drug abuse and alcoholism, and his only wish was to see his little daughter. Reid went in search of the mother and child only to find out Judy Stevens had died several months ago and given guardianship to a friend. The Montgomery woman. What had alarmed Reid was the neighbors' comments. According to Mrs. Fisher, the guardian was flighty, irresponsible and incapable of taking care of a five-year-old child.

Reid was the child's only blood relative, and nothing would prevent him from making sure his niece met her father before he died. He glanced at the absurdly ornate home again, then at the small sign positioned to the right of the sidewalk. Camellia Tea Room—Closed. Whoever this flaky woman was, he would set her straight. His niece wasn't going to be raised by some herbal-tea-drinking, small-town loon.

A car whizzed by on the tree-lined street, breaking his concentration. Time to act. He strode along the narrow walkway and up the wide wooden steps leading to the expansive porch. The old planks complained at his weight. The early-October air was thick with the smell of fresh paint. He raised his hand to push the doorbell, but a flush of anxiety caused him to pause. Maybe this situation required a little more backup than his own determination. He was new at this praying business and had no idea what to say to the man upstairs. He closed his eyes and simply asked for help before pressing the doorbell.

"Help!"

The shout came from inside the old house. His instincts kicked in. He grasped the doorknob and pushed. "Is everything okay in there?"

"No. I need help. I'm in the sunroom at the back."

Reid pushed through into the foyer, his gaze focused on the end of a wide hallway. He moved quickly past the graceful staircase, his boots thudding heavily on the wide-planked wood floors.

"Back here."

The feminine voice drew him to a room off to the right. He stopped and looked in, his brows lifting slightly as he took in the situation. The lovely wide-eyed woman had painted herself into a corner. Literally. She'd failed to plan ahead and now found herself trapped in a corner, unable to escape without ruining the fresh paint.

The woman brushed a loose strand of fawn-colored hair from her face. "You sure got here in a hurry. Floyd said he'd send you over, but I was afraid I'd be here until the floor dried. You're Reid, right?"

He hesitated before nodding. How did she know his name? No one knew him in this small Mississippi town.

"Can you get me out of here? I have to pick up my little girl from school soon."

He nodded again. "But how?"

"I don't know, but I have to get out of here and pick up Lily."

The concern in her voice and the urgency in her deep blue eyes overshadowed his questions. He looked about, but didn't see anything that might extricate her from her predicament. "Do you have any lumber around?"

She squinted at him and screwed her mouth to one corner in a way that made him want to smile. "What?"

He hastened to explain. "A piece of wood, a plank."

"Maybe out by the garage."

A quick trip out the back door revealed a small stack of lumber piled near the driveway. He hoisted a two-by-six and carried it back inside. Pulling up a kitchen chair, he then aimed the plank at the woman. She held up her hands.

"What are you doing?"

"Getting you out. Take the end of the board and place it at your feet."

She gave him a skeptical frown, then did as he instructed. When the board rested on the small patch of unpainted floor, Reid pulled the chair into place and rested the plank on the seat, creating a sloping bridge. After checking to make sure the board was secure, he moved to the edge of the door and grasped the frame, extending his hand toward the woman. "Walk slowly up the board. I'll help you."

She shook her head. "I can't. It's too narrow. I'll fall off and ruin the paint."

"You'll be fine. Go slowly and keep your balance. It's only a few feet, then you can take my hand." For a moment he thought she would refuse, but a glance at the clock spurred her on. She definitely seemed determined not to be late picking up her child.

She placed a tentative step on the wood, then another. Her confidence grew as she moved. He stretched out his hand as far as he could. When she grasped his fingers he shifted his weight, holding firmly until she was near the end, then he slipped his hands around her waist and lifted her off the board. She wrapped her arms around his neck. She was small and soft and warm in his arms, and she smelled of paint and oranges.

He looked into her eyes, the cobalt color capturing his full attention. He'd never seen that color before. Their gazes locked. The blue eyes bored into him, burning through his barriers as if she could look directly into his soul and see his deepest secrets. Fear jolted through his body. He set her down and stepped back, swallowing against the sudden tightness in his throat.

When he dared a look at her again, her eyes were wide with surprise. Had she felt the odd connection, too? He opened his mouth to speak, but she beat him to it.

"Thank you. You're a real-life rescue hero. I can't believe you got here so fast. I only called Floyd a few minutes before you showed up."

"Well, I was actually—"

"I'm Tori Montgomery, by the way. I've got to rush off, but Floyd said you were looking for a job so I'm hoping you'll be my new handyman. I'm afraid I've been driving poor Floyd crazy with all my small repairs. He's completed the remodel I hired him to do, but there seem to be all kinds of little issues with an old house like this. I think I've worn out my welcome by calling him all the time. He suggested I hire a part-time handyman who can be available on short notice. He has too many big projects—paying projects—to keep running over here to fix my old house. I think it was his way of getting me off his back. Of course, I can't afford to pay much. This old house has cost me more than I ever imagined. The opening is several weeks away, but there's a long list of repairs that need to be done before then."

Reid tried to sort through the flood of information she'd given him. She thought her contractor had sent him to be her handyman. The idea took root before he realized it. If he wanted to get the true picture of Tori Montgomery, see if she was the flake he'd been told she was, which right now seemed likely, he'd learn far more from being undercover than telling her outright who he was and what he wanted. He could also get to know his niece. What harm could it do to go along with the error? He was handy, he could help around the old house and maybe find some ammunition to help him secure custody of his brother's child if necessary.

"What would you like me to do first?"

She picked up her keys and faced him. "Oh, great. So you'll help me out?"

The hope in her eyes sent a twinge of remorse along his nerves. He was used to undercover positions, but this wasn't a gang of thugs he was trying to infiltrate. This was a lovely young woman he was deceiving. "Sure."

She smiled and the cobalt eyes took on a new life, full of sparkle and joy. "Then you can start by replacing the old cabinet door pulls and handles with the new ones. They're on the counter. I'll be back soon."

She started past him, then stopped and looked into his eyes. The connection jolted him again. Odd.

"Thanks for the rescue. There are drinks in the fridge if you want one."

Reid watched her walk away. The paint-stained cutoff jeans and the oversize shirt did nothing to detract from her feminine figure. The short ponytail bobbed as she moved like a friendly wave. Tori Montgomery wasn't quite what he'd expected. But she was still a big question mark in the suitable-guardian category.

* * *

Tori Montgomery slid behind the wheel of her small sedan and inserted the key. It was a good thing Reid had shown up when he did, or she'd have been stuck in that corner for hours watching paint dry. How humiliating. She could have called her friend Shelley and had her bring Lily home, but she liked picking up her little girl from school. It was one of the happiest parts of her day, seeing the big smile on the sweet face as she climbed into the car. Besides, she was determined to be the perfect mother, and a mother should pick up her child from school, not expect a friend to fill in for her.

Her gaze drifted to the sunroom extending out from the back of the historic home. Reid wasn't anything like she'd expected. Floyd had referred to him as a young man. But this guy looked to be midthirties. Then again, Floyd was in his sixties, so he'd likely consider anyone under forty young.

There was something unsettling about her new handyman. He'd plucked her from the board as if she weighed nothing, making her aware of the strength in his arms and the broad, sturdy shoulders. He'd smelled so good she'd wanted to nuzzle closer to his neck and inhale the musky scent. He didn't smell like any of the other workers who had filled her house these last few months. Instead of the laid-back, jovial attitude she'd come to expect, Reid was controlled, distant and observant.

He didn't look like them, either. His six-foot frame was sturdy and strong, and perfectly proportioned, like a model from an outdoor catalog. His black-coffee-colored hair had a mind of its own, waving over his ears and falling across his forehead.

But it wasn't his physical appeal that had rattled her. She'd looked into his eyes and been drawn in, looking beyond the rich brown color with the thick lashes to the darkness beyond. He was a man with secrets and deep pain, but he was also searching. She'd felt a quiver of connection in that moment he'd held her. An odd recognition. Something in common. But before she could explore it, he'd set her down and stepped away. The dark eyes shielded anything he was feeling, leaving her with a need to know what he was hiding. He'd assumed an air of control and command that sent a twinge of concern along her nerves.

Now she was being ridiculous.

Jerking her thoughts back into focus, she started the engine and pulled out of the drive. What did it matter how the man looked or if he had secrets? She needed a handyman to stay on top of all the glitches that popped up in her 150-year-old home, and as long as he could do that she was satisfied.

Surprisingly, Tori arrived at the school in record time. Her thoughts had been distracted by the handyman. Inside she took the left hallway to the kindergarten rooms. Her friend Shelley was also Lily's teacher. She was hoping to find a few moments after class to talk to her before she headed home. Shelley's little girl, Emily, was Lily's best friend, and having them live next door had proved a real blessing. The girls spent hours together. It was really very sweet to watch thcm. Having a new friend close by had made Lily's adjustment to moving to Dover easier. Tori thanked the Lord daily for all he'd provided in her new role as guardian and mother.

It was a role she'd accepted at the request of her dying friend, but one she feared she was totally inadequate to handle. She'd never pictured herself as a mother. Never pictured herself as much at all. As the baby girl of the five Montgomery siblings, she'd been spoiled and pampered, but she'd never found her calling. Nothing seemed to hold her attention for long. She'd attempt a new job or a new skill and master it quickly. Then the boredom would set in and she'd go in search of something new to stimulate her mind. Three degrees, six jobs, dozens of crafts and three broken engagements later, she wasn't any closer to finding her place in the world.

That wasn't exactly true. Being Lily's mom had given her more satisfaction, more joy and delight than she'd ever known. It had also filled her with a fear of failure that kept her up nights. What if she made a mistake? What if she wasn't as good a mother as Lily's mom would have been?

Tori stopped at the last door on the right. Her daughter's room.

Daughter. It was still odd to think of the child that way. Peeking in, she saw Lily and Emily at the craft table in the back, putting away the crayons. Shelley spotted her and came forward.

"Hey. How's it going with the old house?" She glanced at the paint stains on Tori's faded cutoffs. "Been wielding a paintbrush, huh?"

Tori chuckled. "Yes, and I made a mess of it. Would you believe I actually painted myself into a corner? I was afraid I'd be late picking Lily up."

Shelley slid a stack of books into the shelves behind her. "I could have brought her home with me."

"I know, but it's my job. I shouldn't pass it off on someone else."

"Now you know that's not how it would be. You're just trying to make a perfect life for Lily, but that's not possible. No one has that. Stop worrying and enjoy your little girl."

"She's not mine. She's Judy's little girl." For the last year and a half, Tori had been living in California with her friend, providing care and support as she battled cancer. With no family, Judy had asked Tori to be Lily's guardian and raise her the way she would have if she'd lived.

"Wrong. You're her mother now." Shelley grinned. "So how did you get out of the corner?"

"Oh. I was rescued by my handyman."

"You have a handyman now?"

"I hope so. Floyd fired me." She hastened to explain. "There's always something around the place that needs to be fixed or repaired, and I've been calling Floyd to send someone over. But he can't keep pulling guys off other jobs, and he's going to start charging me for each call, so he suggested a guy who could work part-time and be on call for all my repairs."

"Can you afford it?"

"No, but I don't have a choice. If I'm going to have the bed-and-breakfast open for Thanksgiving week, I have to get all these repairs taken care of. Having someone on call would be a huge help. I already have four guests lined up. Everything has to be ready."

A little body pushed past Shelley and lunged at Tori.

"Aunt Tori."

A rush of softness coursed through Tori's body as she bent down to hug her little girl. "Did you have a fun day?"

The dark curls shimmered as she nodded enthusiastically. "We made paper flowers. But we can't show you yet. It's for a surprise."

"That sounds like fun. I can't wait."

Lily looked up at her teacher. "Can Emily come to our house and play when we get home?"

Shelley touched Lily's head lightly. "Sorry, kiddo. Emily has a dentist appointment today, but she can come over for a while later."

Lily pouted. "But I'll miss her."

Tori hugged the girl. "You got a new book in the mail today. You can read it until Emily gets home."

"Yay! A book."

"We'd better go. I want to see how the handyman did, and maybe I can get him to take a look at the pocket door that's jammed."

"So about this handyman," Shelley prompted. "Old, young?"

"Oh, he's thirtyish, tall, dark, serious. I'll let you know more if he works out."

"Are you working on the flood committee this weekend?"

Tori nodded. "You?" Torrential rains last week had caused the Pearl River to overflow its banks, leaving serious damage to the west side of town. It had flooded several homes in an upscale neighborhood with four feet of water, but it was the homes farther downriver that had borne the brunt of destruction. The residents there had no insurance, no means of repairing or replacing their homes. Peace Community Church, along with other organizations in town, had formed committees to help pull out damaged walls and floors and rebuild the homes. Sadly, there were enough homes in need on that side of town to keep everyone busy for many weeks. Some had turned their attention to collecting furniture, clothing and household goods for them, as well.

"I did, but I'm not sure how much help I'll be. I've never cleaned out a flooded home before."

"Me neither, but my brother Linc said be sure and wear a mask because the stench is awful."

Shelley grimaced. "I suppose it is nasty work. But I can help."

"Are you sure?" Tori smiled as an image of the fastidious Shelley covered in grime formed in her mind. "I can't wait to see that—Miss Spotless guts a house. I hope you have an appropriate outfit."

Her friend feigned insult. "I've got game. You wait and see."

Tori chuckled. "I'm going to take pictures. I know several people who won't believe it without proof."

They said goodbye and Tori took Lily's hand as they left the building, her thoughts still with the victims of the flood. She counted her blessings each time she thought about the people who had been forced from their homes. It put her problems into perspective. She faced a multitude of obstacles in getting her new B and B up and running, but it was nothing compared to losing everything.

On the ride home Lily regaled Tori with stories from school, funny things she and Emily had done, and speculated on the book waiting for her at home.

Tori was relieved to see that Reid's dark blue truck was still parked at the curb when she pulled into the drive. The thought did cross her mind that she'd left a stranger in her house without a second thought. Then again, Floyd had sent him, so he must be trustworthy and qualified.

Lily scurried ahead through the gate in the picket fence into the backyard. "Where's my book?"

Tori stopped on the walk when she saw the handyman sitting on the porch steps. He looked relaxed and at home. She started to smile, but his gaze latched onto hers and she caught her breath. He was studying her, sizing her up. She could sense his probing intellect reading her.

She sucked in a breath and shook off the sensation. She was being silly. The man had a commanding presence to go along with his chiseled features. His jaw had been cut with a straight edge, his nose even and strong over a generous mouth. The air of intensity and mystery about him was both intriguing and unsettling.

She stopped at the steps. Lily was already there staring. "Lily, this is Mr. Reid. He's going to be helping around here for a while."

"Are you going to fix things? 'Cause we have lots of things that are broken."

Reid glanced at Tori, and the look in his eyes startled her. His mouth softened; his dark probing eyes warmed as he looked at her little girl. "Then I'll do my best to fix them all."

Lily flashed her brightest smile. "Good, 'cause we have bee bees to get ready for."

Tori smiled and rested her hands on her daughter's shoulders. "She means bed-and-breakfast guests. B and B. I want to have the house ready by the middle of next month. Will you be available during that time?"

He looked at Lily. "I think I can work it out."

"Aunt Tori, where's my new book?"

"On the kitchen table."

The girl bounded up the stairs and hurried inside.

Reid met her gaze with raised brows. "Aunt Tori?"

His tone and gaze suggested there was more behind his question than mere curiosity.

"Lily is my ward. I became her guardian when her mother died. Aunt Tori just sort of happened." She faced her handyman and sensed his probing gaze again. He was gauging, trying to figure her out and making a mental list of her good and bad points. She looked away, flushed and uncomfortable. When she glanced back, the probing look was gone and his gaze was unreadable.

Or was she merely being overly sensitive?

It was happening more and more since she'd brought Lily back to her hometown. She questioned her decisions, second-guessed every move and read something negative in others' comments and expressions too often.

He stood. "I finished attaching the hardware. Is there anything else?"

She had a long list, but for some reason she wasn't ready to hand him another project. She took her phone from her purse. "If you'll give me your number I'll call you when I need you."

He took the phone from her hand and their fingers brushed, drawing their gazes together. Had he done that on purpose? He punched in his number. "Call anytime."

"We haven't discussed your pay."

"There'll be time for that later."

"Where are you staying?"

"The Dixiana Motor Lodge. Not far."

Reid nodded and stepped past her, leaving a waft of his tantalizing aftershave in the air. She watched him as he walked away, his slow, easy gait in keeping with his controlled demeanor and his economy of words. She'd never met anyone who stirred so many questions. Nor someone who had caused her nervous system to quake so unexpectedly. A sudden shiver chased up her spine. Had she done the right thing in hiring him?

In the kitchen of the main house, Tori saw the gleaming new cabinet hardware Reid had installed. He'd even placed the old handles in a small box. At least he was considerate.

Picking up the box, she started toward the table where she'd been collecting items to take to the attic later. She glanced at the sunroom and blinked. The unfinished patch in the corner was painted. The evidence of her faux pas was gone. Had the handyman done that? How had he managed? More important, how thoughtful of him to have finished it. She'd have to thank him. His credentials shifted her opinion up a notch. He'd completed the task she'd requested neatly and had even gone the extra mile on the floor. Maybe she'd found the right man after all. She needed someone she could depend on if the house was going to open on time.

Floyd had come through again. He'd sent her a skilled worker to take on all the minor repairs. It was an added bonus that he was easy on the eyes. Which didn't matter a wit. Handsome men were a dime a dozen. All she was interested in were his skills.

Despite that, she still wondered about the odd sense of connection that had passed through them earlier. Her imagination. That's all it was. She'd merely been reacting to being rescued like a damsel in distress.

She was no damsel, and she didn't need to be rescued. But she did need a man who could fix things.

Chapter Two

Reid strode along the tastefully decorated hallway of the Hamilton Haven Nursing Facility in Hammond, Louisiana. It reflected the high level of care they provided and reassured him he'd selected the perfect place for his brother, and it was located only an hour from Dover, which made visiting easy.

Stopping at room 107, he tapped on the door before stepping into his brother's room. The early-morning sunlight streamed through the window, and the scent of fresh linens brought into contrast the difference in Eddie's living conditions since they'd reunited. Reid had tracked him to a small charity hospital in Baton Rouge. He was receiving adequate care for his conditions, but the room was dark and depressing and did little to ease his brother's pain. Eddie had tried to talk him out of spending the money, but Reid insisted. He'd failed his brother in so many ways. The least he could do was make his final days as comfortable as possible. But nothing could make up for his neglect over the years. If he'd been a better, more understanding brother, Eddie might not be dying.

As Reid came in, Eddie greeted him with a feeble smile and raised his hand in greeting. Reid grasped it gently in his. "How's it going, little brother?"

"Good. I have everything I need." He shifted a little on the bed. "I didn't expect to see you so soon. Everything all right?"

Reid had been heartsick when he'd found his brother suffering so. The doctors had told him Eddie had two, maybe three, months before his body gave out. That was six weeks ago, and time was running out. He had to make things right—give his brother the one thing he wanted more than anything else.

Reid took a seat in the recliner beside the bed, leaning forward with his arms on his knees. "I found her. I found your little girl."

Eddie closed his eyes and nodded. "Thank you, Lord. Tell me about her."

"Her name is Lily and she's a little beauty. Long, dark brown hair and big brown eyes."

"Like Mom's?"

Reid paused. He'd never thought about that. "Yes, exactly like hers. And like us, I suppose."

Eddie nodded thoughtfully. "Her mom had blue eyes. And what about the woman who has her? Is she unhinged like the neighbor said?"

Reid chose his words carefully. He didn't want to upset his brother. "She's energetic and a bit unfocused, but no, I don't think she's crazy."

"Is she good to my girl?"

"As far as I can tell, but I've only seen them together for a few minutes."

"Will she bring my girl to see me?"

"I haven't asked her yet. It didn't come up."

"Why not?"

Reid stared at his hands a moment before responding. "I want to observe things for a while, get a handle on her and her relationship with Lily."

"Why?"

Reid had never mentioned the possibility of gaining custody of Lily. "In case I need to step in and change things."

"File for custody, you mean? Is Lily in danger?"

"No, but it wouldn't hurt to know all the

facts before I tell her about you. Besides, shouldn't Lily be raised by a relative?"

"Maybe, but I won't be around and you're a single guy."

Reid pressed his lips together. A single guy who'd spent most of his adult life with the dregs of humanity, which meant he was devoid of the nurturing abilities a child needed.

Eddie studied him a moment. "What aren't you telling me?"

He'd forgotten how Eddie could see through him. He was beginning to wonder how he'd ever worked undercover if he was so transparent.

"There was a misunderstanding when I arrived." He explained his unexpected rescue mission. "If she didn't plan ahead for something like painting a floor, what if she fails to plan ahead for Lily?"

Eddie shrugged off the concern. "That could happen to anyone. So are you going to see her again?"

Reid nodded. "I'm going to be her handyman for the next few weeks."

"And she agreed, knowing who you are?"

Reid sat down and clasped his hands together. "Not exactly." He explained the rest of the mix-up.

"So you let her think you were the handyman her contractor sent?"

"For the time being. This way I can see how they actually interact together and make sure she's taking good care of Lily. Once I'm confident she is, I'll explain and she'll be more likely to agree to let me bring Lily to see you."

A deep frown creased Eddie's frail features. "Reid, for a smart guy, you're being really stupid. You've been undercover too long. You see everything as a mission to take down the bad guys. It's never right to deceive people. It's one of the first things the Lord taught me when He saved me. Mark my words—your deception will only backfire." He shook his head. "I want you to promise me you'll set things straight. Quickly. I don't have much time left."

Reid nodded. "Don't worry, I'll handle it." Eddie might have a point, but the only thing that mattered was making sure Lily was cared for, and if the Montgomery woman wasn't suitable, then he'd have to step in, which meant he had to have evidence and ammunition. But he'd honor his brother's request. He'd come clean soon. All he needed was a few days.

Tori lifted her coffee cup and took a sip, grimacing at the tepid liquid. That was the second cup she'd let get cold this morning. Leaning back in her desk chair, she raked her hair away from her face with a soft groan. She'd been going over the numbers for an hour, and the result was still the same. Her finances were stretched to the max. Every penny had to be accounted for if she was going to open on time.

She'd foolishly assumed her savings and the profit from the sale of her property would be enough to get the B and B up and running. But even with all her calculations, she'd been hit hard by unexpected costs. The plumbing, electric and roof had all needed to be replaced. The discovery and remediation of asbestos and lead paint had further slowed the construction. The remodel of the kitchen in the main house had taken longer than normal because of restoration requirements connected to a historic home. Her contractor had explained that a historic home required special materials at every turn. She couldn't run to the store and buy new molding. It had to be replicated to match what was there.

The funds she applied for would ease her situation considerably. Unfortunately, she still had to wait for the on-site inspection, which wouldn't happen for a few weeks yet, and then she'd have to wait several more weeks for the funds to be applied. The only thing keeping her afloat at the moment was her online jewelry-design business, but that covered only food and utilities for her and Lily.

She'd have to tighten her belt a while longer and concentrate on getting the inside of the rooms decorated and arranged for future guests. She had invested everything in this venture. It was her future—and Lily's. The business would not only provide a living, but would allow her to spend as much time with her little girl as possible. But at this rate, it would never happen, and she would be stuck with a half-done white elephant of a house and be forced to take an eight-to-five job, put Lily in after-school care and miss out on so much of her life. She'd promised Judy she would be a good mother to Lily. The mother Judy would have been, and she intended to keep that promise, no matter what.

"Morning, Aunt Tori."

Tori's concerns melted into mist at the sound of the child's greeting. She spun in her chair and opened her arms. "Good morning. How's my little sweetie pie this morning?"

"Good." She climbed into Tori's lap for a hug and a snuggle. "I dreamed about a big flower that came to play with me in the yard."

"You did?"

"It was blue and pink. Oh, and I dreamed about a little puppy with floppy ears."

Tori stifled a giggle. Her little charge had been angling for a pet since they'd arrived in Dover four months ago. She suspected it had something to do with all her new cousins having dogs. "Maybe we can get you a puppy after we get our B and B open."

"But that's forever."

"Not really. Are you ready for breakfast?" Mornings were Tori's favorite part of the day. Lily generally woke up soft and sweet and cuddly, and they enjoyed breakfast together before leaving for school. But today her thoughts were focused on her bank account.

By the time she had dropped off Lily and returned home, the sorry state of her finances had given her a monster headache. One thing was clear: hiring a handyman now was out of the question. She'd have to learn to make minor repairs herself or rely on her family. Unfortunately, they all had busy lives of their own and weren't able to drop everything and come running. Besides, she'd received enough help from them. She needed to provide for Lily on her own. Time was running out, and there was still so much to do.

First off, she had to unhire a handyman.

Tori dialed Reid's number. It went straight

to voice mail. She considered leaving a message telling him she wouldn't need his services after all, but it seemed rude to fire him over the phone. Instead, she simply asked him to come by the house to speak with her.

A small tingle of anticipation skittered along her nerves. Seeing the man again wouldn't be an unpleasant experience. He was very appealing. His muscular frame, his probing brown eyes and cool mysterious demeanor were right out of a book. Something on the order of Mr. Darcy, or maybe Mr. Rochester. She shook off the idea. Maybe it was a good thing she couldn't have him as her handyman.

Telling him she couldn't hire him would be awkward considering how enthusiastic she'd been when she'd offered him the job. She hoped he wouldn't be upset. She had the impression that Reid was a man capable of fierce emotions, which might explain why he was so controlled. But she also sensed a loneliness behind his eyes, as if he was searching for something. Or she could be creating drama in her mind. It was a bad habit of hers.

Reid still hadn't returned her call by the time she'd picked up Lily from school.

"Can I take my new book out to the glider?"

"Of course." Lily had been overjoyed to receive a new book, and she loved to read in the old double-glider swing.

"Will you watch me?"

"Of course." Settling onto the back porch in one of the old wicker rockers, she smiled as her daughter skipped across the grass and climbed into the glider. Since arriving in Dover, Lily had developed a need to have Tori near or at least watching over her at all times. Tori loved watching the child play. She was endlessly entertaining, and Tori delighted in everything the little girl did. However, sitting and watching her made working difficult. She'd transferred several items to her tablet so she could oversee Lily's playtime and still get work done. The amount of paperwork involved in opening a bed-and-breakfast was staggering. Every time she submitted one completed document, three others would be required.

The squeak of the gate told her someone was there. She looked up as Reid came up onto the porch, his solid footsteps sounding on the wooden floor. He stood with one foot on the porch floor, one hand grasping the post, an expectant look on his angular face. His presence sent a wave of awareness along her nerves. He was an impossible man to ignore. When he stepped into a room he sucked all the air and energy right out of it. Very peculiar. She stuffed the weird notions away and stood. "Thank you for coming."

"No problem. I had an appointment this morning. What's up today?"

"Nothing, I'm afraid. I've been going over my financial situation, and I'm unable to afford to hire any extra help. I'm sorry. I offered you the handyman job before I'd looked at my bank balance. Things should turn around in a few weeks, but until then I'm tapped out." She smiled, hoping to lighten the news. Reid's dark eyes narrowed, and his brows drew together. Her heart skipped a beat. Even a deep frown couldn't mar his chiseled features.

"That's too bad. I was looking forward to the challenge."

"And I could use the help. By the way, thank you for finishing the floor. I didn't notice it until you'd left yesterday."

"The paint was quick to dry. Half hour tops."

How had she not known that? Probably because she'd failed to read the information on the paint can. He must think her a real ditz. She touched her ear. "So I could have walked out of the corner and not smeared the floor?"

He shrugged.

Was that a smirk she saw move his lips? She crossed her arms over her chest. "Well, thank you again for rescuing me and for completing my paint job."

"You're welcome." He turned to go, but the post under his hand shifted loose. "Was this on your repair list?"

"One of them." Her lists grew longer every day.

"Hey, Mr. Reid."

Tori saw her daughter waving frantically. She climbed out of the double-glider swing and raced across the yard, stopping in front of Reid. "This is my new book. You want to read it to me?"

Tori watched the big man carefully. Would he refuse? Or would he acquiesce to the little charmer's request? She stifled a grin when Reid shot a panicked glance in her direction. Before she could respond, Lily tugged on Reid's finger and urged him to sit on the step.

"I'll turn the pages, okay?"

Slowly Reid lowered his tall frame to the wooden step. Lily flashed a big smile as she handed him the book, then burrowed under his arm, balancing her elbow on his thigh. Tori watched the broad shoulders ease and the hard line of his jaw soften. No one could resist her Lily.

The sound of his deep, soft voice sent a warm tremor through her heart. Behind that dark cloak of mystery he wore was the heart of a kind man. She'd like to know more about him.

What was she thinking? There was no time for any kind of relationship. She had her hands full raising Lily and running her business.

She glanced at the pair on the steps. Lily snuggled close as Reid spoke the words softly. It would be nice to have someone to share her life, her work.

She shoved the thought aside. Her track record in the romance department was abysmal, and she vowed to avoid all personal relationships going forward. And fantasizing about them, too, for good measure.

Reid read the simple words of the book—a story about a baby squirrel separated from his mother—all the while aware of the sweet child snuggled against him. His brother's little girl. The thought settled deep inside, stirring up unfamiliar emotions. A tiny hand reached out and awkwardly turned to the next page. Lily grinned up at him, then settled back down. He focused and went on with the story. "'Why are you out all alone, little squirrel?' asked the big black bird."

"No, Mr. Reid. You have to say it different. Like this."

Lily lowered her chin and repeated the words in a deep voice, drawing a soft chuckle from his chest that he hadn't expected.

"The bird is a meanie. So you have to talk like a meanie when you read him."

Her sincerity was both amusing and amazing. He knew nothing about kids. But he knew this little girl, Eddie's child, was undoubtedly smart beyond her years.

He managed to finish the book with the appropriate voice changes and received a kiss on the cheek from Lily that left a fuzzy, warm sensation in the center of his chest. Before standing, he watched her skip back to the swing.

Miss Montgomery was leaning against the railing watching Lily, and the look of love on her face brought a soft glow to her skin. He had no doubts about her affection for his niece, but there was more to consider. She'd admitted financial trouble. That gave him concern. He needed a little time to get a good read on the situation. He needed the handyman job to keep him close by. It was the perfect cover.

His conscience pinged. Eddie was right. He shouldn't be lying to her, and he'd tell her the truth soon. He'd rather have a better understanding before he came clean, though. A couple days, at least.

"Miss Montgomery, I have a suggestion if you'll hear me out. I don't mind helping out around here until things improve for you. We can settle up when you're able."

"I can't ask you to do that. Besides, why would you want to work for free?"

Reid rubbed his temple. A plausible story quickly formed in his mind, only to be overlaid with his brother's reprimand. Eddie was right again. He'd been working undercover for so long that lying came more easily than telling the truth. He needed to get a handle on this right now, and keep as close to the truth as possible without revealing his true relationship with Lily. "The fact is, I left my last job. I needed a change. I thought a small town would be a good place to start. The work I'd do around here would allow me to sharpen my rusty handyman skills."

"What did you do before?"

Reid chose his words carefully. "I was in law enforcement."

"Oh. My brother is a police officer here in Dover. I know how stressful it can be. I can understand your need for a new direction. I felt the same way when I became Lily's guardian. But I'm finding changing course harder than I expected. I thought buying this place would be the answer. I wasn't prepared for all the unexpected problems."

"You bought this place because of Lily?"

She nodded. "I had to make a living, and I thought that opening a bed-and-breakfast would allow me to provide for her and still spend time with her. Unfortunately, it's not working out the way I'd hoped."

She needed him, and he pressed his advantage. "Miss Montgomery, I meant what I said. I'd be happy to help around here for a few weeks."

She crossed her arms over her chest and faced him. "How would you feel about working for room and board?"

"I'm listening."

"The small building behind the main garage is actually a studio apartment. The girls converted it for their older brother."

"Girls?"

"Ada and Edna Smiley. Camellia Hall was their family home for generations. The apartment hasn't been used in a long time, but it's larger than the motel room you're currently in. You can take your meals with us. I'm not the best cook in town, but you won't starve."

It was the perfect solution and more than he'd hoped for. "All right. I have to admit the Dixiana is getting smaller by the day."

She nodded. "Flo runs a good business, but Dover needs more options for visitors. It's either the tiny cabins at the motel or the high prices at the Lady Banks Inn. I want to offer another option. Something more reasonably priced and comfortable than the formality of the inn."

He extended his hand to seal the agreement. "We have a deal, then? Room and board in exchange for work." She hesitated a moment, then grasped his hand. Her fingers fluttered in his palm. Did he make her nervous? He looked into her eyes and felt the jolt again, a strange kind of connection he'd never experienced before. She possessed an energy that vibrated through her fingers. And he found it intriguing.

She broke eye contact, tugging her hand from his. "You can move in as soon as you like. I'll find the key and get it to you."

"There's still half a day left. What can I do next?"

"There are several doors that won't shut and windows that won't open, and the pocket doors between the two parlors are stuck."

"I would have thought your contractor, uh, Floyd, would have taken care of this."

"He would have, but it was one of many things that got cut from the budget. There were roof leaks, foundation repairs, termites, plumbing problems and electrical issues. Which didn't leave any room in the budget for anything else."

"How much work do you still need to do?"

"Small things here in the main part of the house. The original plan called for upgrades in the living quarters where Lily and I are. And a complete remodel of the tearoom on the other end of the house. I'd hoped to keep it running to bring in a little income, but that's on hold now." She motioned him to follow her. "Let me show you what needs to be done. None of the doors in the living quarters close completely."

He gestured for her to lead the way, following her to the end of the hall to a door marked with a small plaque that read Private. It resisted when she pulled it open. "This one is the worst."

He made a note to start with that door. He followed her through it, his mood lifting considerably. He'd managed to convince her to keep him on as handyman. The offer of room and board had been more than he'd expected. He could see how Lily and Tori interacted without it seeming like he was spying on them. Which was what he was doing. He'd manipulated her into keeping him around.

Eddie's warning surfaced again. A few days, that's all, then he'd come clean. Once he was sure Tori was a responsible guardian, he'd explain everything. Hopefully, by then, they would have established a good relationship, and his request to take Lily to see her dad wouldn't be an issue.

Tori stopped in the living area, which was one large room with a small kitchen tucked against the back wall beside a narrow staircase leading to the second floor. A comfy sofa was placed invitingly in front of a charming fireplace. French doors on either side led out to the wide porch. He was struck by how welcoming the small space was. "Nice place."

"Thank you. This corner of the house used to be the servants' quarters. It's the perfect size for us. We'll be spending most of our time in the main house, hopefully entertaining lots of guests, but this will be our own private retreat."

A sudden image of him and Tori cuddled on the sofa flashed into his mind. He shut it down. "Do these doors work?"

"Yes, but the bedroom doors upstairs could use some work, as well."

Reid's gaze drifted to the far corner of the living room and the desk there. Something sparkled, and he stepped closer. Boxes of flashy jewelry cluttered the top. Several large pieces were spread out on a felt board and held in place with pins. "What's all this?"

"My custom-jewelry business. I take old brooches, pins and necklaces and rework them into statement necklaces and sell them online."

"A woman of many talents."

"Right now all I want is to get ready for my guests."

"Those bee bees Lily mentioned?"

She smiled, and Reid couldn't help but notice it was brighter than the jewelry she worked on. Something about Tori made you feel welcome and accepted. His conscience flared. He'd spent years living a lie, pretending to be someone he wasn't, but it had never felt like this.

Eddie was right—he'd been undercover so long he'd lost touch with who he really was. He didn't want to lie to Tori any longer, because he was beginning to see the extent of damage his ill-conceived deception might cause. He suddenly dreaded the look of condemnation he'd see in her pretty eyes when he came clean. Oh, what a tangled web—it needed to come down today.

Tori hurried back into the main kitchen, stopping briefly on the porch to check on Lily.

She was still sitting on the glider swing with her book. Tori studied her a moment. She seemed subdued today. Not her usual cheerful self. Was she missing Judy? Since bringing Lily here to Dover, the little girl had experienced several setbacks as she grieved. The incidents had rocked Tori's already shaky confidence, making her question again if she was suited to raising her friend's child.

Lily must have sensed her watching because she glanced up, then waved. Tori waved back, praying Lily would eventually accept her mother's passing and embrace her new life here in Dover.

Reassured, Tori moved into the kitchen. The newly remodeled room met all the codes for a professional kitchen and, with the help of her decorator, still reflected its 1870 origins. The small breakfast room off the back connected with the sunroom and would provide a cozy dining space when there were few guests. The formal dining room at the front of the house would be used when the rooms were full, hopefully during most of the fall and winter. Today she planned on going through the three sets of fine china the girls had left with the house and decide which one would be her statement pattern.

Light tapping on the back door pulled her

around. Shelley waved and stepped inside, followed by two little ponytailed girls. Lily skidded to a stop, vibrating with excitement.

"Can I show Emily my new bookcase?"

Her new lavender scalloped-edge bookcase had arrived a few days ago, and she'd spent an afternoon putting the books in just the right spots. "Yes, but Mr. Reid is up there working on the doors so don't get in his way, and then come back down and play in the sunroom so I can see you, okay?"

Lily tossed a "'kay" over her shoulder as she and Emily dashed toward the living quarters.

Shelley settled on a stool at the counter. "Mr. Reid?"

"The handyman."

"You hired him?"

"Sort of. We agreed he'd work for room and board temporarily. He's going to stay in the apartment. This way he'll be available whenever I need him."

Shelley frowned and leaned forward. "You're telling me you hired a stranger, who's also going to live in your apartment? Tori, what were you thinking?"

"He's not a stranger exactly. Floyd recommended him. He's nice. A bit solemn and mysterious, but he does good work and he's eager. He finished painting my floor without being asked." Tori pulled a glass from the cupboard and filled it with the Smiley girls' famous mint iced tea and set it before her friend. "It's only for a few weeks. Once I have some funds I'll pay him and hire a professional to finish the work."

Giggles and thumping sounded before Lily and Emily burst into the main kitchen. Reid was right behind them. He stepped into the room and nodded. "All the doors work. They only needed a little adjusting."

"Oh, Reid, this is my friend and neighbor, Shelley Vinton."

Reid nodded. "Emily's mother. Nice to meet you." He faced Tori. "What's next on your list? I can't start the windows until I pick up replacement materials."

"How are you with pocket doors? The one between the two parlors is wedged into the slot. Floyd wasn't sure they could be restored. I'll show you."

Shelley's expression was beyond curious when Tori returned. She braced herself for a flood of questions.

"*That* is your handyman? Tori, he may be a lot of things, but a handyman? Really?"

"What are you talking about?"

"I've hired a few in my day and they never

looked like him. Did you notice the biceps on the man?"

Not only had she noticed, she had first-hand knowledge from when he'd plucked her from the makeshift bridge he'd used to rescue her. "He used to be in law enforcement, so of course he'd be strong."

"I hope you know what you're doing. That man is dangerous."

"What are you talking about?"

Shelley placed her hands over her heart as she batted her lashes. "Guard your heart, girl-friend."

Tori rolled her eyes. "You forget this heart has been closed for business for a while now."

"If you say so. Oh, I saw the list of volunteers for this weekend. With all that help, we should have those flooded homes ready for carpenters by the end of the day. Maybe you should ask for volunteers to help with the B and B."

"In exchange for what?"

"A free night's stay when you open, or a romantic night for two."

"Not a bad idea, but the clock is ticking and I'm nowhere near ready to open. I still have decorating to do, a registration desk to set up, marketing, the menu. I don't know when I'll be able to reopen the tearoom."

"Maybe you shouldn't. You said the girls had shut it because business had dried up."

"The Camellia Tea Room is part of the home's history. I'd hate to see it end."

"And when would you have time to run that and the B and B, too?"

Tori sighed. "I know. Too bad I can't clone myself."

Shelley patted her arm. "What you need is a partner. Someone to work with you here, to share the load and give you moral support. Someone who would care as much as you do."

Tori sent a warning glare at her friend. "Stop right there. I know what you're doing. Every time you see an attractive man you start hinting. I'm not going down that path again. Third time wasn't a charm, it was a disaster. He lied to me about everything. Lily is my life now. There's no room for anyone else."

Shelley smiled and picked up her purse. "Not even a very intriguing handyman who's right under your nose?"

Tori pointed to the door. "Take your sweet child and your sweet self and move along please. There's nothing to see here."

"Fine. I'm going."

Her friend's heart was in the right place, but her suggestion wouldn't work. Although now that Shelley had planted the seed, the idea of having a partner began to take root…

Reid aimed the flashlight into the slot encasing the old pocket door. Something was jammed between the door and the wall, but he couldn't see it or reach it. He tried tugging the door back and forth to dislodge the blockage. When the stubborn door refused to budge, he stepped to the opposite door and applied the same technique. His efforts were rewarded when the door slid outward a foot, bringing with it a thick strip of insulation.

A little more tugging produced more insulation and a few more inches of exposed door. If insulation was the culprit on the other door, and if he could remove it all, the doors might slide closed. Barring any mechanical problems, in which case he'd have to do more research. For some reason he wasn't quite sure of, it was important for him to fix one of Tori's concerns.

It was obvious, even in the short time he'd been around, that Tori was determined to get her bed-and-breakfast open on time. And her motivation, to give Lily a stable home where she could spend as much time with her as possible, was reassuring. His conscience flared again. He had to come clean and tell her who he was and why he was here. His concerns about Tori being a suitable guardian had all but disappeared.

Reid cocked his head when he heard a strange noise coming from the kitchen. It sounded like crying. Then he realized—Lily was sobbing.

He hesitated, then made his way down the hallway to the kitchen door. He stopped, catching his breath at what he saw. His employer and her little girl were seated at the round breakfast table. Lily was sobbing uncontrollably as Tori cradled her in her lap, making comforting noises.

"But Miss Shelley said Emily was going away. I don't want her to go. Mommy went away."

"Emily isn't going away, sweetheart. She's going to her grandma's, the same way you go to visit yours. She'll be back in a few days."

"But Mrs. Fisher said Mommy went away. Will Mommy be back, too?"

Reid watched the tears flow down Tori's cheek as she brushed the dark hair from Lily's face. "No, sweetie. Remember we talked about how sick Mommy was and how her body was too tired to keep working?"

Lily nodded. "She's in heaven with Jesus and she's happy."

"That's right. And now you're here with me and I'm very happy to have you and we'll be a family. Just you and me."

"And our bee bees?"

Tori smiled. "Yes, and our guests. You'll be a big help to me. You can help me make them feel very special, and they'll want to come see us again and again."

Lily snuggled close to Tori, her little fists hugged up against her chin while Tori stroked her hair.

Reid moved quietly back from the door, his chest twisted into a hot, uncomfortable knot. But the area around his heart felt strangely soft. If he'd had any doubts about Tori taking care of Lily, they were put to rest now. She loved the little girl. Wasn't that all that mattered?

He rubbed his forehead. He'd tell her today before he left. Before he moved in. Once she knew who he was, he might be fired—again.

"Reid."

He spun around to see Tori, with Lily in her arms, staring at him, both of their eyes moist and cheeks pink from tears. A rush of protectiveness slammed into him. He cleared his throat. "I was coming to report on the pocket door." He didn't want Tori to think he'd been spying on them.

"Can you fix it?"

"Maybe. It's jammed with insulation, but if the hardware isn't damaged it should be a simple matter to oil it and get it sliding smoothly again."

"That's a relief. It's a feature guests love."

Tell her. He stared at her.

"Was there something else?"

"I'd like to talk to you when you have a moment."

"All right, but it'll have to be later. I need to spend time with Lily, and I have some paperwork that has to be submitted first thing tomorrow."

"No problem."

Tori kissed her child's cheek before setting her on the floor. "Lily, you go on to your room. I'll be right there." She handed him a key. "I meant to give you this earlier. I'm afraid the apartment might be a mess."

He held up his hand. "For a free room, the least I can do is clean it."

He took a step toward her. "Is Lily all right? I didn't mean to eavesdrop, but I heard her crying and... Does she get that way often? Missing her mother, I mean."

Tori rested a hand at her throat. "It's been a long time since her last spell. Thankfully, they're becoming fewer and fewer. Her mother and I tried to prepare her for the loss, but she's so little she doesn't really understand. How do you explain to a five-year-old that her mom is gone forever? I feel so helpless and inadequate."

He searched for something to say. He hated to see her so full of doubt, but comforting a distraught woman was out of his comfort zone. "I thought you handled it exactly right."

She shook her head. "I wish I could do more for her. It's moments like this that make me wonder if Judy did the right thing in giving me custody."

Reid impulsively touched her arm, wanting to reassure her. "I think she made a good choice. You're the perfect guardian for little Lily."

She looked at him with appreciation in her cobalt eyes, but evidently her self-doubt still lingered. Now was not the time to reveal his identity. "I'd better get back to the pocket doors."

"Thank you." She straightened and offered a

slight smile. "Oh, would you take a look at the faucet in the upstairs bath in the living quarters tomorrow? The water flow is a trickle. Oh, and Jimmy Ray will be here, too. He's going to start painting the living quarters."

"I'll look at it first thing in the morning. And if it's all right I'll move into the apartment this evening."

"That's fine. Let me know if you need anything."

"I'll do that."

Reid worked on the door a while longer, until it was obvious he needed something more than his hands to clear out the insulation. He'd have to pick up a hook and rent a Shop-Vac. Beyond that, he had some research to do. And an explanation and an apology to prepare.

Seeing Tori so insecure had been unsettling. Didn't she see how strong and capable she was? Her love and affection for his niece couldn't be questioned.

He couldn't continue this subterfuge. It would hurt all of them.

Because there was something vulnerable about his new boss. Outwardly she took charge like an engineer on a mission, but inside she

was filled with doubts. He suspected someone had hurt her deeply. And the last thing he
wanted to do was hurt Tori any more.

Chapter Three

Reid's encouraging comment earlier kept replaying in Tori's mind. He'd felt she'd done a good job in calming Lily and comforting her. She wished she felt as confident. She second-guessed her handling of Lily every moment. Her mom assured her all mothers felt this way, but Tori wasn't convinced. The women in her family all seemed like supermoms. Linc's wife, Gemma, raised two children and ran a successful event-planning business. Gil's wife, Julie, was the mother to three—Gil's daughter, Abby, and three-month-old twins. Her sister, Beth, owned her own dance studio, raised her stepdaughter and taught classes while pregnant. Even her brother Seth's new bride worked full-time, studied for her degree and took care of Seth's son, Jack. Sometimes she wondered if she would ever measure up.

They tried to reassure her that she was doing a fine job, but for some reason, Reid's encouragement meant more than all the others combined. What was wrong with her that the simple compliment from a stranger held more sway than those from her family?

All she needed to do was focus on getting the business open on time. With Reid close by to handle the long list of repairs, she was free to start concentrating on the details. Decor, menu, schedule and, of course, there was the paperwork and documentation. Things she hadn't considered when she'd bought the old home.

Opening a bed-and-breakfast wasn't a simple matter of inviting people to come and stay at your house. The state regulations were overwhelming: business licenses, restaurant license, liquor permit, even if she would only be offering wine. And with each requirement came an inspection. Being listed on the National Register had brought with it another to-do list. She was grateful Floyd was aware of the guidelines and had consulted with Laura Holbrook, a local restoration specialist, to make sure everything was acceptable.

Strange thing was that all her previous jobs were proving to be a blessing. She'd worked in her mother's Real Estate office as a sales agent, the family Electrical business as an accountant and she'd owned her own flower shop briefly and even tried her hand at interior design. Now, all that experience would give the skills she needed to run the B and B.

Glancing out her bedroom window, she saw the light in the apartment, reminding her she now had a boarder. Reid had moved in this evening. She felt bad she hadn't been able to clean up the place and figured she could at least provide him with fresh linens.

After a quick check on Lily to make sure she was sleeping soundly, Tori gathered a set of clean sheets and towels and carried them to the apartment. The sweet strains of a Chopin nocturne seeped through the door as she approached. Classical music? Not what she'd expect from a stoic guy like Reid.

He opened the door quickly when she knocked, his dark eyes locking onto hers and sending a quiver down her spine. He wore a faded T-shirt and dark warm-up pants that only emphasized the muscular chest. Her mouth went dry and her palms dampened. *Oh, my.* What was wrong with her? She'd never had this kind of reaction to a man before. Coming here was a dumb idea. His dark eyes suddenly softened, and his mouth arched on one side. Not exactly a smile, but more of a slight lifting.

"Evening."

She cleared her throat and thrust the items toward him. "I thought you might need these."

"Thanks, but that wasn't necessary."

She glanced around the small space. He'd removed the dust covers and rearranged a few pieces of furniture. A worn duffel bag and a small satchel were on the bed in the alcove. "I forgot to mention you can have weekends off, unless of course some major catastrophe comes up."

"Good. I have a standing appointment on Sundays I can't miss."

She wanted to ask what it was but resisted. He probably had a girlfriend someplace. "Is there anything else you need?"

"Not a thing."

He took a step toward her, and she became acutely aware of his height. When he'd set her down from the board the other day, her head had rested right below his chin. She remembered thinking how perfectly she fit in his arms. Her cheeks flamed when a glint appeared in his dark eyes. Had he guessed what she was thinking? She forced a smile, searching for something to say to break the awareness arcing between them. She couldn't stop looking at him, and each time she did she wanted to smile like a kid with a crush on the boy next door. "I thought I'd make you a list of the things that need fixing in case I'm not around. Then you can scratch them off as you finish them."

"Good idea."

Their eyes locked again and she became aware of his scrutiny. Her heartbeat skipped. What was he looking for? She broke contact and moved to the door. "Oh, don't forget our deal includes meals, so I usually fix breakfast at seven. Help yourself to whatever is on hand for lunch. Supper may vary, but normally we eat around six or so."

He followed her, stopping close enough that she could feel the warmth of his body. Her gaze zeroed in on his chest, watching as it rose and fell with each deep, steady breath. She turned her attention to his voice. He was saying something.

"I'm not much on breakfast, but coffee would be good."

"There's always a pot ready." He rested his hands on his hips and she had the feeling he wanted to say more. He had mentioned he wanted to talk to her about something.

"How's Lily? No more tears?"

"No, she's been her usual happy self since then."

He hesitated a moment. "What about Lily's father? Where is he?"

All her defenses shot into place. Her fingers curled into fists. Her jaw worked side to side as she tried to temper her response. She took a step backward. "I don't know, and I don't want to know. He has no place in Lily's life. Judy never wanted him mentioned to Lily. *Ever*." She turned to leave but Reid took her arm.

"Why?"

"Because he's a heartless, selfish coward who abandoned his child." She pulled free of his grasp. "I need to get back to Lily."

She sensed Reid's intense gaze on her back as she strode to the house. From the way she'd exploded, he probably thought she was a lunatic.

After a quick check on her daughter, Tori went downstairs to her craft table. Working on her jewelry designs always calmed her down and cleared her mind. Putting the glittering pieces together to create a lovely necklace gave her satisfaction.

Fifteen minutes later, residual anger still vibrated along her nerves. Any mention of Lily's father churned up a fierce need to protect.

She'd probably overreacted to Reid's question, but any discussion of Lily's worthless parent never failed to infuriate her. Especially now that Judy was gone. It was up to her to honor her friend's wishes, and after hearing how that man had abandoned her friend when she was pregnant, she could understand why Judy would become enraged whenever the topic came up.

Still, that was no reason to snap at Reid. She'd have to get used to the question being asked. It was only normal for people to wonder when she showed up in her hometown with a little girl to raise. Thankfully, that didn't happen often. Most everyone knew her and her family, and the reasons behind Lily's presence had already been through the rumor mill, everyone's curiosity satisfied.

She'd apologize to Reid in the morning… if he was still here. She hoped she hadn't chased him away, because she really needed his help around here. Maybe she'd make the Smiley girls' cinnamon rolls in the morning as a peace offering. She'd been meaning to try the recipe. She was hoping it would become one of the hallmarks of her business. Warm. Sweet. Comforting.

The very essence of what she wanted Camellia Hall to become.

* * *

The morning air was thick and muggy, suggesting a thunderstorm brewing for the afternoon. Reid crossed through the dew-damp grass, weighing his options on how best to approach Tori. He'd been unprepared for her fierce reaction to his question about Lily's dad. His shock had shifted quickly to defensiveness. She was talking about his brother. Eddie might deserve his fair share of condemnation for his behavior, but Tori's bitterness ran deep. It might ruin any chance he had to take Lily to see his brother.

When Tori had knocked on his door, he'd just finished talking to Eddie and assuring him Tori was a good mother to Lily. He'd felt certain he could convince her to take the little girl to see him soon. Now he might have to backtrack. Her reaction didn't bode well for a family reunion.

Eddie was right. His little undercover operation had backfired big-time. He had made things worse. He had to tell Tori the truth before she found out some other way.

Inside the main house, Reid inhaled the welcoming aroma of fresh coffee and cinnamon rolls. Tori and Lily were nowhere to be found. Her car was still in the drive along with a contractor's van, so she must still be in the living quarters. He took his time savoring the hot, dark liquid and the sticky sweet rolls. Another perk to living on the property. He hoped he could continue working here. He was growing attached to the place, and to Tori and Lily.

He'd slept soundly despite his troubled thoughts about Tori's outburst, but his concern had been there to nag him when he'd awakened. He'd planned on talking to her today, hoping her reaction last night was simply because he'd caught her off guard. Something told him that wasn't the case, however.

Sufficiently caffeinated, Reid hoisted his tools and started toward the living quarters. Before he could knock on the door, she opened it. Lily waved and smiled. Tori looked professional today, in a dark slender skirt and a light blue blouse. Lily, her hair held back with a wide band, wore striped pants and a little shirt with a princess on it. Both looked adorable.

"Good morning. Did you find the coffee and rolls okay?"

"I did."

"I have to run some errands this morning after I drop Lily off at school, but I'll be back around lunchtime. Jimmy Ray is painting the living room so you might have to work around him."

"No problem."

"Oh, and there's sandwich fixings in the fridge for lunch, so help yourself."

Lily tugged on his hand. "When I get back will you read me another story, Mr. Reid?"

He hunkered down, a rush of warm emotion circling his heart. "Sure thing. I'll be right here." He'd hoped tracking down his family would bring him peace. He'd never imagined that he would find it in the bright eyes of a five-year-old child. Except his niece belonged to Tori, and he had no connection to her at all. Yet.

Lily bounced on her toes with happiness. "You're a good reader."

He'd received his share of recognition during his years as an agent, but none had given him the satisfaction found in Lily's sweet compliment. Eddie's child was special. He would be so proud. He looked at Tori. He had to tell her who he was and why he was here. Once she heard the full story, she'd change her mind.

After the ladies left, Reid made his way to the living room in the private area. The furniture had been shoved toward the center of the room and drop cloths spread on the floor in front of the wall to be painted. A gray-haired man was hunkered down stirring a can of paint. He glanced up and smiled, coming to his feet.

"You must be Reid, the handyman Miss Tori took on. I'm Jimmy Ray Fuller." He extended his hand.

"Fuller Painting Contractors. I saw the van. Nice to meet you. Will I be in the way working on the window sashes?"

"Not at all. I'll come back and paint the trim later. So what brings you to our little town? Dover is off the beaten path."

Reid placed his toolbox in front of the window before answering. The question made him uncomfortable. Probably because he'd chosen to hide his real reason for being in the small town. His cover-up stirred his conscience into a bitter swill. Something else new in his emotional library. He formed his answer around as much truth as possible.

"I left my old job and I wanted to start fresh. A small town seemed like a good fit for now." When Jimmy Ray didn't respond, Reid faced him and found him staring, a knowing glint in his pale blue eyes.

"You're a former cop, aren't you?"

Reid frowned. "How could you know that?"

"It takes one to know one." He ran his hands over the paint roller to remove excess lint. "And I'm guessing you did a lot of undercover work, am I right?"

Reid could only nod. What was it about the people here—Tori, and now Jimmy Ray—that they could see right through him? When had he become so transparent? If he'd been this way on an assignment, he'd have been dead years ago. "DEA."

Jimmy Ray nodded. "I was undercover with the Memphis PD. It took its toll. I left and came to Dover. The wife was from here."

"And you became a painter. That's a far cry from police work."

"I needed something stress free, something I could start and finish and see results. Law enforcement never seemed to get better. It felt hopeless. I wasn't making a difference." He gestured to the walls. "With this job, I come in, do my job, the customers are happy and I don't take the work home or lose sleep over it."

"Sounds good. I suppose that's what I'm looking for, too. A life that doesn't keep dragging me down."

"Well, if you stay on here you'll come to enjoy it. Especially being around Miss Tori. That young woman has a gift for making people feel at home. She's going to be a terrific hostess when this place opens up."

He agreed, but he still had concerns. "Do

you think that'll happen? She says she's having financial issues. I'm working for room and board."

Jimmy Ray brushed the comment aside. "For now, but she'll sort it out. I'm working for free. My version of a housewarming gift. I'm close with her family. Knew her since she was a baby and I want to see her succeed. She's had it rough lately, and I admire her for taking on the little girl all alone. That child has given her a purpose that was lacking in her life."

"I assume there's no boyfriend in the picture?" The back of his neck suddenly burned. What was up with him?

"Are you fishing, Reid?" Jimmy chuckled. "She is a pretty lady. No, I don't think she's looking for any kind of relationship. After three failed attempts, I think she's only focused on Lily."

"She's been married before?"

"No. Engaged. Three times. She called them all off."

Jimmy went to work on the wall and Reid turned his attention to the window, locating the access pocket and starting the replacement of the inner workings. When the window slid up and down easily, he moved upstairs to work on the three windows up there. His thoughts were distracted by what Jimmy had shared. Why had Tori broken off three engagements? Was she that poor a judge of character? Or was she incapable of making a long-term commitment—and what might that mean in regard to Lily? Would she grow tired of being a parent and abandon his niece? Absurd. He refused to believe that. From what he'd seen, Tori was devoted to his niece, despite her own confession to feeling inadequate as a mother. Yet it did raise questions in his mind.

He'd promised himself he'd talk to Tori soon about his real identity, but now he wondered if he needed to observe the situation awhile longer. A day or so. But no more than that, because it wasn't fair to her or Lily.

With the sashes repaired, Reid gathered his tools and headed downstairs. He opened the door and caught sight of a man entering the main hall at the same time he heard Tori's voice in the kitchen.

"Floyd, how nice to see you."

Reid froze. Floyd. Her contractor.

"Thought I'd drop by and see how you were doing."

Instinct told him to run. He could make it out the back way before Floyd saw him. He took a quiet step toward the back door. Tori was speaking excitedly to the man.

"Wonderful, thanks you to. Reid has proved invaluable. He's fixing all the doors that were stuck, and today he's working on the windows."

Caught like the rat. One look from Floyd and his cover would be blown.

His shoulders sagged. He should have told Tori sooner. He'd never wanted her to find out like this. He wanted to tell her when the time was right, on his own terms. Not when he'd be exposed like a criminal. He eased back away from the door. He could slip out through the French doors. His conscience clawed at his mind. This was wrong on so many levels, but if his identity was revealed now, Tori would probably fire him on the spot, and he needed time to prepare her for the truth. Safely behind the wheel of his truck, he cranked the engine and pulled away.

Coward.

Strange how he'd faced situations like this every day when he was undercover. Slipping away to avoid detection had kept him alive. But this felt different. He'd never been ashamed of what he did on the job, but the hot, smothering shame he was experiencing now was unbearable.

Tomorrow. He'd come clean tomorrow. If

he approached her in the right way, he knew he could make her see his side of things.

His cell phone rang, the caller's name displayed on the dashboard screen. Eddie. Reid exhaled a troubled sigh. For a moment he considered ignoring the call, but he couldn't risk it. He pressed the accept button. "Hey, bro. Everything okay down there?"

"I'm good. I wanted to know if you'd told Tori who you are?"

The whole world was working against him today. "No, not yet. I've been busy making repairs."

"Reid, don't wait any longer. Please. I want to see my little girl, and I don't know how much time I have left."

Reid's eyes stung. "I know, little brother. I promise I'll settle this soon." He debated whether to tell Eddie about Tori's reaction to his inquiry. He didn't have the luxury of waiting for the right time or softening blows. "Eddie, I asked her about Lily's dad the other night and she became very angry. Does she have reason to be so bitter toward you?"

The long silence made Reid regret his question.

"Probably. I ran out on Judy when she told me she was pregnant. I never called her after that or asked about the baby. Yeah, she would have been angry. Judy had a temper and she was capable of carrying a grudge."

"Apparently, that carried over to Tori."

"Are you saying Tori won't let Lily come see me?"

Reid set his jaw. "No. I'll handle it. You lay back and take care of yourself. I'll work it all out. I promise."

Reid had just made a promise to his brother that he had no way of keeping. He had to get on top of this situation before it all exploded in his face.

Chapter Four

Saturday morning dawned bright and warm. A rare cold front had dropped the normally balmy October temperatures into the fifties the last few days, but today the forecast called for low seventies. A blessing, considering she'd be working at the flood houses today. She wasn't sure what she'd be doing, but she was positive it would be dirty, messy work. She dug out her oldest jeans and shirt for the job. Lily was all packed up and ready to spend the day with Tori's mother.

"Lily, let's go, sweetie."

The little girl dashed into the room, her arms folded around half a dozen books. "I'm taking my favorites to Grandma's so she can read to me."

"That's a good idea, but do you know Grandma has all kinds of books there she can show you? Maybe you'd like to see all the new ones and leave these here at home."

Lily thought a moment. "Okay. Will the doggies be there?"

"I don't know. We'll see when we get there." Lily had started pushing hard for a dog of her own. Tori was holding off as long as she could. She wanted to research the various breeds and find one perfectly suited to her little girl.

After leaving Lily with her mom, she headed to the south end of town and the narrow street along the Pearl River that had been inundated with flood waters. The sight of the ravaged homes broke her heart. None of the houses were large, but each one represented a place for a family to live. Now they were all soaked and everything inside destroyed. How would they ever return to these dwellings?

She and Shelley were assigned hauling duty. They pulled out the ruined belongings and piled them at the curb. The mounds of debris lining the street were heartbreaking.

She was grateful for the mask provided because the stench was nauseating. After hoisting a waterlogged sofa cushion, she tossed it on the pile. Her attention landed on the man working in the house next door. Something about those broad shoulders, that posture, was familiar. He turned and her heart skipped a beat when she recognized Reid. He smiled and raised a hand in greeting before disappearing inside the building. What was he doing here? Had Floyd told him about the community project?

Shelley plopped an armful of soggy linens onto the pile. "What are you staring at?"

"My handyman. He's working in the house next door."

"Really? Cool."

"But how did he know to come here? I didn't tell him."

"I guess Floyd must have."

"But Reid has only been in town a week."

"So? He's already getting involved in the community. That's impressive. Handsome and compassionate, to boot. Sounds like a good catch."

Tori glared at her friend, who was smiling gleefully. She had to admit, she hadn't expected Reid to be the community-service type. He was too reserved and aloof. Yet here he was, right in the thick of things.

Tori went back to work, but each time she went outside her gaze traveled to the other house, searching for a glimpse of her handyman and wondering if there was more to his volunteering than met the eye. Her last relationship had proved to be a lie on all levels. Will had pretended to love her, to be CEO of a large corporation and a Christian. His deception had left deep scars and caused her to question everything about the men she met.

As if materializing out of her thoughts, Reid stepped out onto the porch carrying a large bookcase. It was nearly as tall as he was, yet he handled it like it was Lily's little lavender one. Unable to look away, she admired the way his muscles flexed as he maneuvered the large piece of furniture to the curb. He glanced over and caught her staring.

He set the wooden furniture on the pile, then started across the soggy yard. Her mouth suddenly went dry. She cleared her throat to find her voice. "What are you doing here?"

"Same thing you are. Helping out."

"How did you know about the workday?"

"Jimmy Ray invited me."

She should have guessed. Jimmy Ray was always recruiting volunteers for one thing or another. "I thought you had personal obligations on weekends."

"I do. On Sundays. I thought I'd spend my first day off lending a hand. I'm not good at sitting around doing nothing."

She could well imagine a man like Reid

going stir-crazy with nothing to do. "Well, thanks for helping. How's it going?"

"We're ready to start on the carpet and dry-wall in this place. Should have it cleared by lunch. Lily at her grandma's?"

"Yes. I'll pick her up when I'm done here. Oh, several of the spindles on the front porch are loose. Could you take a look at them?"

"Add them to the list. I'll check them out first thing Monday."

"Thanks. I'd better get back to work." She moved off, aware of Reid's gaze on her back. She always felt as if he was analyzing her, but she had no idea why. Was he interested in her, or was he wary of her? Neither made sense. She was hardly a threat to anyone, least of all a big man like Reid, and she certainly wasn't looking for any romantic entanglements. Tugging her ball cap more securely to her head, she shook off the fanciful ideas as nothing more than her heightened suspicious nature. She had to get over that. Not everyone was like Will.

But she had to admit that something about Reid intrigued her. He floated through her thoughts more times than she'd care to admit. Fatigue. That's all it was. Too much on her mind, and he was a pleasant distraction. Nothing more.

She started back to the house as Shelley trudged out the door with a bag of trash. The sight of her oh-so-fussy friend covered in streaks of dirt and grime made her smile. Pulling out her phone, she snapped a quick picture, only to receive an angry glare in return.

She waved her phone in the air. "This will go viral in ten minutes. Tabloids will pay big bucks." As she started up the porch steps, she caught a glimpse of Reid and another man wrestling a ruined refrigerator off the porch and to the street.

She really had to get a grip.

Reid noticed the dark gray sedan in the drive the moment he stepped out of the apartment Monday morning. He didn't recognize it. Perhaps it belonged to one of Tori's siblings. He'd yet to meet the Montgomery clan, but Tori mentioned her family frequently during their conversations. From what he'd gathered, the family was close and Tori was particularly close to her sister, Bethany, and her brother Seth, the cop. He found himself looking forward to meeting them. If he was still working here.

After attending early service yesterday at Peace Community, he'd spent Sunday with

Eddie, who had been tired and depressed, worrying about living long enough to see his daughter. Reid had promised to come clean with Tori today. No more procrastination. He'd deliberately waited until she'd come back from taking Lily to school. Hopefully, whoever was at the house wouldn't delay his conversation.

He jogged up the porch steps and entered the back hall, turning toward the kitchen, where he usually found his landlady enjoying another cup of coffee as she organized her day. She had her back to him and spun around when he entered. The greeting on his lips died when he saw she wasn't alone. An older man with craggy features and a thick head of gray hair stared at him. Floyd. He'd only caught a glimpse of him before. The look in his eyes raised the hair on Reid's neck. A sign he knew meant trouble. He braced himself. The look of betrayal in Tori's blue eyes pushed a hot barb deep into his conscience.

The older man had one hand on the counter, which slowly curled into a fist. "You must be Reid."

He knew a setup when he saw one. He nodded, preparing himself for the inevitable.

"I'm Floyd Mason, her contractor. Miss Tori

was telling me what a big help you've been around here."

"I'd like to think so."

Floyd crossed his arms over his chest in a challenging posture. "Imagine my surprise when the man I sent to help her, a twenty-something kid named Sylvester Reed, called me last night to apologize for running out on me and going back to Arkansas. Now, who are you and what are you doing here?"

Chapter Five

Reid froze, his heart slamming painfully against his rib cage. This was not how he'd wanted Tori to find out who he was. The stunned expression on her face twisted his insides. He prayed she'd let him explain. Though, after this, it might not matter. Eddie was right—he had made a stupid, impulsive decision to deceive Tori, and now he was going to face the music.

Floyd took a menacing step toward him as if to place himself in front of Tori.

Tori had a hand resting at her throat, her eyes filled with confusion. His throat clenched when he saw fear rise in her dark blue eyes and the pulse in her neck speed up. He knew she was thinking the worst. He wanted to reassure her that he wasn't going to harm her, but he couldn't blame her for being wary.

There was no reason to lie. He could see now how Tori had made her assumption. But how would she feel when she heard his name? "My name is Reid Blackthorn." He looked at Tori, but she didn't react. Hadn't she heard what he'd said? Or maybe she didn't recognize the name. She'd made it clear Judy never mentioned Lily's father, and Judy went by her maiden name.

"That doesn't answer my question. Who are you and why are you hanging around here?"

Reid directed his answer to Tori, who was anxiously chewing her bottom lip. He could only imagine what she was thinking. At the very least she'd probably labeled him as some kind of lunatic or an opportunist waiting to take advantage of her or—worse yet—a danger to Lily. He had to reassure her, but he wasn't ready to tell her the whole truth with Floyd watching. "I told you the truth. I'm a former DEA agent looking for a fresh start. I had stopped to ask directions when I saw the Camellia Tea Room sign, then realized it was closed. That's when I heard you call for help." His chest tightened at how easily the lies came to him. *Lord forgive me.*

Tori closed her eyes and looked away. Reid had never felt lower in his life.

* * *

Tori took a deep breath, trying to calm her quaking nerves before looking at Reid again. How could she have been so gullible, so careless? She'd hired this man on faith alone, not bothering to ask for references or even his last name.

"Why did you let me think you were Reed? I mean the one Floyd sent?"

He glanced off before answering. "It occurred to me that working as a handyman would be a good way to try out a new line of work. I'm afraid my undercover instincts took over, and I didn't consider the repercussions of withholding information."

Her internal lie detector screamed. Why hadn't it gone off earlier when Reid first showed up? Hadn't she learned her lesson with Will? She was normally so cautious, but somehow Reid had slipped past her sensors.

Floyd squared his shoulders. "Would you like me to escort this guy off the property?"

It was on the tip of her tongue to say yes. *Get him out of my sight.* But another part of her wanted to hear the truth. She needed to understand how she'd been so drawn in. Not to mention redeem some of her self-respect.

"Thank you, Floyd, but I'll handle this."

"Are you sure? I don't like leaving you alone with some stranger."

"It's all right. Besides, Seth is only a call away. He'll be here with sirens blaring if I need him." She saw Reid flinch. The moment Floyd left she wondered if she'd made another mistake in letting him leave? If Reid was here to rob her or harm her, he'd had plenty of opportunity. But he was guilty of something, and she wanted to know what he was up to.

Reid was staring at the floor, obviously embarrassed at being found out. She crossed her arms over her chest. "Why didn't you tell me there'd been a mix-up? I was desperate for help. I probably would have given you a chance."

"I realized that, but by then I was making repairs and you were in and out and busy with Lily." He shrugged.

Her lie detector vibrated again. "What aren't you telling me? I can see it in your eyes. You're hiding something."

He took a breath as if preparing himself, and slipped his hands into his jeans pockets. "You didn't recognize my last name?"

"No. Why should I?" The look in his brown eyes sent a shiver down her spine. Whatever he was going to say wouldn't be good.

"Because I'm Lily's uncle."

It took a moment for his words to register. Lily's uncle? "That's not possible. Judy didn't have any siblings."

Reid took a step toward her, and she backed away, confusion and alarm swirling in her head.

"My brother, Edward Blackthorn, is Lily's dad."

His words refused to register in her mind at first. They were so preposterous. "No. You're lying again. He walked out on her and no one knows anything about him."

He touched his chest. "*I* know. I tracked Judy down, and from there I found you and Lily. Didn't Judy ever tell you the father's name?"

"No." Tori rubbed her forehead. "She always referred to him with some derogatory term, never his name. She'd become enraged whenever she talked about him. I quit asking because it made her so upset." A javelin of fear pierced up through her being. "Is that why you're here? To try to take Lily? Well, you don't have a prayer of gaining custody. I'm her legal guardian. Judy wanted me to raise Lily. She's mine."

"And she's *my* niece." Reid inhaled a deep breath before looking at her. "I'm not trying to take her away."

"Then what do you want?"

"I want to take her to meet her father."

Tori glared. Was he out of his mind? "No. Never. Judy was adamant about never telling Lily about him. As far as Lily is concerned, she doesn't have a father."

"Is that fair?"

"Fair? Was it fair for that man to walk out the minute he found out Judy was pregnant? He left her alone to have a baby and raise her without any emotional or financial help. He never contacted her, never asked about the baby. She hated him."

"I'm not defending what my brother did."

"There is no defending his actions."

"Agreed, but the circumstances have changed."

"Nothing has changed. Except now I have a traitor in my home. I never would have let you work for me if I'd known."

"I know."

She spun around, arms hugging her waist protectively. "I think you'd better go."

"Tori, let me explain. I have a good reason."

"There can't be a good reason. Judy wanted Lily protected from any knowledge of her father and what he did. I promised to do the same."

"Tori, my brother is dying. He only has a

short time left. A month, maybe less. All he wants is to see his daughter before he dies. Is that too much to ask?"

"Yes."

Reid ran a hand across the back of his neck. He was obviously getting agitated. She stiffened her resolve.

"Eddie regrets what he did and he knows he could never make up for it, but all he's asking is to see her."

"Out of the question. There's no place for him in her life. And there's no place for you here. I think it's best if you leave." She forced herself to ignore the hurt in his brown eyes. That wasn't her problem.

"Tori, I'm no threat to you or Lily. I meant it when I said I wasn't trying to take her away, but she's my family. I'd like to spend more time with her."

"You should have thought about that before you lied to me. I can't forgive lying. Ever."

"All right. For now. But please think about what you're doing to Lily. She should know who her father is."

"No, she's better off not knowing. I'll figure out what I owe you and you can come by and pick up the check."

"I don't need the money. Keep it."

She shook her head. "I don't want to be indebted to you in any way."

"Fine."

She could see he was exasperated. Too bad. The one thing she couldn't tolerate was being lied to. Yet it kept happening. What did that say about her?

Reid turned and left. The moment he was out of sight, her knees started to buckle. She sank onto the stool. She hated confrontation, and he'd forced her to stand her ground. But she'd had no choice. Judy's wishes had to come first. But his brother was dying. She hadn't expected that. A small swell of sympathy bloomed. She smothered it with a memory of Judy and her fierce plea to protect Lily at all costs.

She owed it to her friend. A promise shouldn't be broken.

Reid didn't bother to pack his things. He'd come back for them later. He climbed into his truck and headed for Hamilton Haven. He had to tell Eddie about his screw-up. His brother would be so disappointed. Not to mention heartbroken and probably angry. Thanks to him, Eddie might never get to see Lily now. Any hope he had of convincing Tori to relent was gone. She hated them both.

The drive to Hammond dragged on forever. Reid kicked himself with every mile that rolled over on the odometer. His feet moved like lead as he crossed the parking lot, entered the building and stopped at his brother's door. *Lord, give me the words to say. Help me make this right.*

He tapped lightly on the door before entering. Eddie was propped up in bed and the TV was on. He must be having a good day. If it wasn't for the IV in his arm and the steady beeping of the monitors he'd look normal, though much older than his thirty-two years. His hard living had taken a massive toll on his system.

"Reid. Why are you back so soon? I didn't expect to see you until next weekend."

"Yeah, well."

"What happened?"

The worry in his brother's eyes knotted his stomach. He pulled up a chair next to the bed, searching for the right words. "My cover was blown. The contractor found out I wasn't the guy he sent, and he told Tori, who was not happy to learn that not only had I lied to her about being the handyman but—" he paused, dreading the words he had to say "—that I'm Lily's uncle."

"And I'm her father. How did she take it?"

"Not well. She didn't even know your name."

"Oh. I guess Judy hated me more than I thought." Eddie laid his head back on the pillow, his disappointment obvious.

Reid rested his hand on his brother's arm. "I'm sorry, bro. It's all my fault. I messed up. I should have been honest from the beginning."

"No. This is on me. I'm the one who ran out on my wife and child because I was afraid to face the responsibility of a family."

"Why didn't you follow up? Check on them?"

"Fear. At first I didn't want to face her anger. Then after a while it seemed easier to ignore them, pretend it never happened and lose myself in chemical oblivion." He reached out and patted Reid's hand. "I let you down, too. I messed up my life good."

Reid shook his head. "No. I promised Mom I'd look out for you, and instead I ran off to the service and never turned back."

"You couldn't have changed anything. I was bent on a path of self-destruction and no one could have stopped me."

"Tori is determined to do what Judy wanted, and that means keeping you out of her life."

"Are you going back?"

"Not sure. She said she'd let me know when my pay is ready. I don't need it, but I do need to pick up my stuff. I'm sorry, Eddie. I ruined it for you."

"The blame's mine. I can't expect you to fix a mistake I made years ago. Would you try to do me one favor, though? If you do talk to her again. Ask her if you can take a picture of Lily so I can at least see what she looks like?"

Reid's heart sank. Why hadn't he thought of that before? He'd had ample opportunity to take pictures of Lily, and he felt sure Tori wouldn't have minded. "Sure. I'll make it happen." How, he had no idea.

"What's wrong with me?" Tori dabbed at her teary eyes with the tissue Shelley had given her. She'd asked her friend to come over as soon as she got home.

Her friend squeezed her hand. "Nothing."

"Then why do men lie to me? Do I have a sign on my forehead that says *I'll believe anything you tell me*?"

"Don't be silly. Not all men lie to you. Reid did tell you mostly the truth."

"But not the most important part. That he's Lily's uncle."

"If he'd told you, would you have hired him?"

"Of course not."

"Exactly. What if you were in his position,

learning you had a niece you never knew about, worrying about your brother who was dying and not sure if she was being cared for? Wouldn't you want to see for yourself? Check things out?"

"Whose side are you on?" Her friend had a point, but she didn't want to acknowledge it.

"Yours and Lily's. I mean, I get why Judy was so angry. I would be, too, but denying Lily even has a father is a bit much, don't you think? And freaking out whenever his name was mentioned?"

Tori buried her face in her tissue. It hurt to admit that her friend might be right. She hadn't allowed herself to question Judy's position on Lily's dad. She'd always given her the benefit of the doubt, especially since she was in a battle for her life and worried about the future of her only child. But none of that overrode her promise.

"When I agreed to become Lily's guardian, I gave Judy my word that I would raise her little girl the way she wanted. I intend to keep my promise."

"That sounds very noble. But what if Judy's way wasn't best for Lily?"

"How can it not be? She was her mother."

"Every woman has a vision of the kind of mother she will be. The reality of motherhood is very different. Raising kids is hard and scary and confusing, and you never know from moment to moment if you're doing the right thing or totally messing up your child. You do the best you can. And every child is different, with different needs. Judy might have had dreams of Lily becoming a dancer or a scientist, but that doesn't mean she would want to be those things."

"Are you trying to depress me even more? Because you're doing a great job."

"I'm only saying don't try to do what you think Judy wanted. Do what you think is right for Lily."

Tori met her friend's gaze. "Honoring her mother's wishes is best."

Shelley nodded. "Okay, but what are you going to do about your handyman? I have a feeling he won't walk away from his only niece so easily."

Tori had the same concern. "I'll tell him his check is ready. Once he picks it up we'll be done." She glanced at her friend, whose skeptical expression called her out. "Truth is, I've called everyone I know, every contractor, every professional and part-time handyman in Dover, and none of them can help me. They all expect to be paid."

Shelley giggled. "Gee. Imagine that."

Tori waved off the sarcasm. "I know. As much as I hate to admit it, I need Reid to help if I'm going to get this place open on time."

"Sounds to me like you might have to eat a little crow."

Tori dropped her chin into her hands. "I don't think I have a choice. But if he agrees to return, there will be very clear parameters set. And he'd better not cross them."

"If he does you can sic your family on him. I've got to go. Let me know what happens, and call if you need to talk again."

An hour later, Tori clawed her fingers through her hair and groaned. She was sunk. Until her reimbursement funds arrived, she was living on jewelry money. She was supposed to open in a month, but she still had so much to do, and with so many repairs necessary, she'd never make it.

Reid was her only option.

She'd never liked the taste of crow.

The text from Tori had come first thing this morning, two days after she'd asked him to leave. Your check is ready.

He spent the last few nights in Eddie's room, and they'd reminisced about the good days before their parents were killed. Eddie reminded him of the childhood dream they'd had of getting a cabin on a lake and fishing their days away. What he wouldn't give for the opportunity now.

Eddie had been very forgiving about Reid's messing up the situation with Tori, which only spurred him on more to fix things. Somehow, he had to appeal to Tori's caring nature. She wasn't a heartless person, just a woman loyal to her friend and determined to grant her requests. But she also loved Lily and genuinely wanted the best for her. Wasn't knowing her father the right thing?

Reid parked at the end of the drive at Camellia Hall, a knot of concern forming in his chest. He had no idea what kind of reception he'd get. He wouldn't put it past her to sock him one. He braced himself for the worst as he took the back porch steps to the door and knocked firmly. It opened, and his breath caught at the sight of her. She was as lovely as he'd remembered. Her light brown hair was hanging to her shoulders, making her eyes look bigger and brighter and framing her delicate features. She wore a pair of slim-fitting slacks and a flowing top that brought out the deep blue of her eyes.

Cool it, man. He cleared his throat.

"Hi." Lame. So lame.

"Hello. Come in."

He stepped into the back hall and followed her to the main kitchen. She picked up an envelope from the counter but didn't hand it to him. He tried to think up some scenario in which she'd have to hire him back. But making up tales had created this situation. He waited for her to speak.

"I have a proposition for you."

This was promising. "I'm listening."

"I find myself in an awkward position. I need to get my business opened on time, and to do that I need to have repairs made. The inspection from the commission is scheduled for next week. If I don't pass I won't get my funds, and without those I can't open. It seems finding a handyman who will work for room and board is more difficult than I expected."

Reid's spirits ballooned. She needed him. And he needed to be here. "You want me to come back on the job?"

"Yes. But there's a new stipulation."

He didn't like the sound of that.

"You are forbidden to speak about Lily's father, and you have to forget about getting my permission to take her to see him. Is that clear?"

It would complicate things, but he'd work with it. He still believed, given the right motivation, that he could convince her to let Eddie see his child.

"All right. And I have one request of my own. I'd like to take a few pictures of Lily, maybe a video I can show my brother. He at least deserves to see what she looks like."

For a moment he feared she would refuse him even that. But he watched her cobalt eyes soften and lighten as she made her decision.

"Fine. But you have to check with me first before you do."

"Deal." His hope was renewed. She started to hand him the envelope, but he pushed it back toward her. "Keep it. We'll settle up when the bed-and-breakfast is up and running."

"I don't think that's such a good idea. I don't want to be—"

"Mr. Reid, you're back! I missed you."

Lily dashed into the room, a book under her arm, and grabbed his leg with the other. A warm bubble of lightness swelled his chest. No one had ever been glad to see him. Except his mom—but that was a long time ago. He rested a hand on her head, gently stroking the silky dark brown hair. "I missed you, too, Lily."

He glanced at Tori. Her expression was a mixture of tenderness and concern.

Two little brown eyes looked up at him. "I got a new book today. Will you read it to me?"

Tori closed her eyes. "I'll read it to you later, Lily."

"No, I want Mr. Reid to do it. He's a good reader."

Reid fought the wave of love flooding his being. In a few short days, his little niece had captured his whole heart. "What's the book about, Lily?"

"It's about a little boy and his daddy going on a fishing trip. Did you go on fishing trips with your daddy?"

"Many times."

"Aunt Tori, how come I don't have a daddy?"

Reid froze. He heard a soft gasp from Tori. "We'll talk about it later. How would you like to help me with my jewelry today?"

Lily smiled and bounced on her feet, causing her pigtails to swing. "Can I pick out the most sparkly ones?"

"You can make your own special necklace."

"Yay! I want to make a blue one." Book forgotten, Lily left the main house and headed for the living quarters.

Reid faced his landlady. "We have more to discuss, Tori."

She raised her chin in defiance. "No, we

don't. There's a list of repairs on the counter. If you'll excuse me, I need to spend time with my daughter."

He watched her go, stiff-backed and hurting. He'd never meant for it to turn out like this. He had to make her understand. He'd agreed to her rules, but he'd also promised his brother he wouldn't fail him again. One of those things would have to be ignored.

He glanced at her list. The pocket doors were number one. He'd already picked up the things he needed to complete the job. Might as well start there.

An odd sense of contentment settled on his shoulders as he began tugging out the remaining insulation from the door channel. He'd grown fond of the old house and wanted to see it spit polished and ready for those bee bees Lily talked about.

Mostly, though, he'd grown fond of Lily and Tori. He wasn't ready to walk out of their lives yet. And he suspected it had more to do with his feelings than the promise to his brother.

Chapter Six

While Lily played with the jewelry, Tori questioned herself yet again about rehiring Reid. Seeing him again had sent her heart racing. Something about his dark brown eyes drew her to him, made her want to learn more about him. She needed therapy. She was far too trusting, too gullible. She should have sent him packing and never looked back.

After sitting down at her computer, she had pulled up her jewelry website to check orders, but her finger clicked on her email, instead, bringing up the one from her brother Seth. After Reid's true identity had been exposed, she'd needed to know exactly who he was. He could be making it all up, though for what reason she couldn't guess. Maybe he was a con artist out to—what? Scam her out of an old house in need of constant repair? The idea was preposterous. Reid had been nothing but helpful and hardworking. Still, she'd been fooled once before by a charming man.

"Look what I made." Lily held up her latest design. "I made it all blue and purple. My favorite colors."

"Lily, it's lovely." Her compliment earned her a big smile from her daughter. She'd awkwardly wired four broaches together. Though gaudy and featuring shades that didn't quite work, the clustered brooches had an interesting symmetry. It touched her deeply that Lily wanted to create alongside her.

"Can I take a book to Mr. Reid now?"

Lily didn't seem to have any qualms about Reid. She'd taken to him from the start. In fact, she'd taken to all the men in the Montgomery family. Perhaps because she'd never been around many men. Was that a good thing or not? Judy had kept Lily insulated from a lot of things in the outside world. If it hadn't been for Tori taking Lily on outings, the little girl would have never left the apartment. Tori had assumed it was because Judy wanted Lily as close as possible during her last days.

"We'll see. Why don't you make me another necklace first."

Tori refocused on the email, seeking reassurance.

He's exactly what he told you. A former DEA agent. Decorated, respected and never in any trouble. He quit eight months ago after a mission went south and he was injured. From all I can find out, he's a good guy.

She closed the file. Except for being the brother of the man who'd ruined her friend's life.

Seth's confirmation of Reid's identity had helped ease some of her fears, but it did little to alleviate her concerns about his intentions. He said he wasn't seeking custody of his niece, but he could change his mind, especially if he decided she wasn't a fit guardian. Did he think she was doing a poor job of raising his niece? She couldn't allow those thoughts to take root. She had enough worries as it was.

The calendar beside the computer reminded her of what was important. Thanksgiving was fast approaching, and she needed Reid to get a lot done. That's all that mattered. As long as he stuck to their agreement, everything would be fine.

Her only other threat was the way her stomach fluttered whenever she looked at him. Obviously a weakness she had to master quickly. Just because a man was handsome and appealing didn't mean she had to develop feelings for him. She'd already had her three strikes, and she was out of the romance game for good.

Tori stood and walked to the desk, placing a kiss on the top of her little girl's head. "You keep making pretty necklaces. I'm going to talk to Mr. Reid."

"Can I come?"

"No. Not yet." Tori stepped into the main hall and peeked into the kitchen where she'd left Reid. Empty. Scraping sounds from the parlor alerted her to his whereabouts. He was hunkered down working on the bottom of one of the pocket doors, which was now fully extended. He glanced up, his brown eyes locking with hers, and she wondered if he looked like his brother. How much of Lily was inherited from the Blackthorn side? Clearly, she had the family brown eyes. They were the same as Reid's. Was it a trait from their mother or their father?

Clearing her throat, she refocused. She saw questions in his eyes and a glint of hope.

He stood, his solid frame suddenly making her feel smaller than her five feet three inches. Despite his deception, she'd never had a moment's concern about her safety.

"I think we have this side in good shape. I'll oil the tracks top and bottom so it'll slide easier. The other side is more stubborn. I'm afraid the top track might be broken, which would mean finding a replacement from the same era and maybe removing part of the molding."

"I think you should know I had my brother check you out."

His dark eyes widened. "Did I pass?"

"According to him, you are a well-respected former agent. So why did you leave?"

Reid wiped his hands on a rag before tossing it into the toolbox. "I'd had enough. My last assignment was rough, and somewhere along the way I realized I wasn't making a difference anymore. No matter how long I stayed undercover, no matter how many dealers I helped put away, there was always another to take his place. I wanted something different. Something not stained by evil and greed. I wanted peace. Family."

"So you decided to come looking for your niece?"

"I didn't know I had one. In fact, I didn't know where my brother was. We hadn't been close since our parents were—died. It took a while to find him, and that's when I learned he'd been married."

"They were never married."

Reid raised his eyebrows. "Okay. At any rate, he told me about Judy and that she'd had a child. He wanted to find them and try to make up for what he'd done."

"Make up?" She took a second to get control of her anger. "No. There's no way he can make up for running out on her, leaving her penniless and alone with a baby on the way."

"He's aware of what he's done."

"So now he wants to step into Lily's life as if nothing has happened? Judy would never agree to it."

"Tori, my brother is dying. He's made a mess of his life and he's paying the price for it. When I found him, he was in a charity hospital receiving barely adequate care. I moved him to a place where he would be treated well and be comfortable in his last days. All he asks is to see Lily. He's in no position to try to get custody."

"Neither are you."

Reid set his hands on his hips and paused a moment, as if gathering his thoughts. "When I tracked down Judy, I learned she'd passed away and left her child with a friend. The woman in the next apartment, a Mrs. Fisher, led me to you. But she made a point of telling me she felt you were unsuitable to care for my niece."

Tori exhaled a sharp breath. "Oh, I can well imagine what the old busybody told you. I was too loud, we laughed too much and we left Judy alone too often. I kept Lily entertained—we played and laughed, and I took Lily to the museums and playground and a whole lot of other places to keep her from seeing her mother waste away. Judy insisted I make each day as fun as possible. But that old biddy across the hall thought because Judy was dying, I should tiptoe around her and pull down the shades and start mourning before she was even gone."

Tears welled up in her eyes. "She fought so hard to conquer that savage disease. But she wasn't strong enough."

"I'm sorry you had to go through that, but I'm grateful you were there to comfort her and help Lily. I knew shortly after I met you that you weren't like Mrs. Fisher said."

"Then why didn't you come clean?"

Reid scratched his jaw. "Well, I had a few doubts along the way. Like painting yourself into a corner, learning you'd had a string of jobs and fiancés. I wanted to be sure before I told you who I was."

"So you *were* thinking of trying to take Lily from me."

"It was in the back of my mind. But not anymore. I had you checked out, too."

"You what?" The nerve of the man. "There's nothing to find in my background."

"Nothing criminal, but you don't come across as the most reliable sort. Always jumping from one thing to another. A restraining order against a former fiancé."

"He wouldn't accept we were through."

Reid rubbed his forehead. "All I want is for my brother to see his child. Nothing more."

"Not happening. I can't. Judy wouldn't approve."

"Aunt Tori, I got tired of waiting." Lily entered the room and smiled up at Reid. "Can you read me my book now?"

Reid looked at Tori for permission.

She set her jaw and took Lily's hand. "He's busy. I'll read it to you. Wait for me in the kitchen."

She started to move away, but he took her arm. There was no threat in his touch, only a firm grip to get her attention.

"Does this hatred of my brother extend to me, as well? Are you going to forbid me to visit Lily, to take her to the park or the zoo? Am I going to have supervised visits?"

"I don't know." She saw the hope fade in his dark eyes, and her conscience flared. Could she in all fairness hold him accountable for what his brother had done? He'd admitted they hadn't been close for a long time.

With a regretful shake of his head, he showed her his back and returned to working on the pocket door. Maybe she should reconsider her position. If it were solely up to her she might relent, but it wasn't. This was Judy's decision and her last request.

She would *not* change her mind.

The unfamiliar scraping sound drew Reid outside his apartment Friday morning and toward the garage. The door was up and he could see Tori attempting to fight her way through a large pile of chairs. They hadn't spoken since their confrontation a day and a half ago. The repair list she'd left in plain view on the kitchen counter every day had been enough to keep his focus on his work. He'd avoided eating supper with them last night and gone to a diner on the square in downtown Dover instead. He had a lot to think through, and the two females in residence at Camellia Hall were too distracting.

Their conversation had dimmed his hopes. He'd seen no hint of relenting in Tori's cobalt eyes. She was loyal to a fault. An admirable quality normally, but it was turning out to be a giant obstacle to his mission. Somehow, he had to get through her wall and make her understand the importance of his request.

Lending a helping hand might earn him a few points. "Good morning."

She barely glanced over her shoulder as she tugged on a small metal bistro table. "Morning."

"You need some help?" He grinned inwardly, knowing she wanted desperately to refuse but wouldn't.

"I'm trying to pull out all the rocking chairs."

He stepped forward and lifted the table out of the way. "What is all this stuff?"

"Outdoor furniture. Mostly the porch rockers and the bistro tables from the tearoom."

She brushed hair off her forehead, and Reid found himself admiring her lovely face. She was naturally attractive. She rarely wore makeup, and her creamy skin glowed when she was excited about something. She had her hair in a ponytail again today, and it swung back and forth as she moved. She had a way of making even the oversize T-shirt and khaki shorts look incredibly feminine.

"And you want them where?"

"The front porch. I want it looking nice when the inspector comes. The bistro table and chairs can stay here. But I think there's a couple of porch swings in the back over there." She gestured in the direction of the far right corner.

"Inspector?"

"From the commission."

"Oh, right. You mentioned that."

"I received a grant from the Historical Society. They provide matching funds to people restoring old homes and businesses. But they work on a reimbursement policy. I have to have the work completed first and provide documentation. Then they'll send an inspector for an on-site assessment. I was notified he'll be here two weeks from Saturday for the walk-through."

"Consider it done."

"Thanks, but I also need you to make sure the porch railings are all fixed. I want everything feeling safe and secure when the inspector arrives."

"Will he be looking for those kinds of things?"

"No. He's only coming to make sure the plumbing and electric and the other repairs meet with historic guidelines, but it wouldn't hurt to have everything in great shape."

Reid tugged out one rocker near the front and shifted a chair to lift a second one. "This one has loose arms. I'll check each one to make sure they're safe. They could use some paint, too."

"That may have to wait. I'll settle for clean and repaired."

"Okay. I'll rent a power washer. It'll make the job go faster."

"I don't have the money to rent any equipment."

"Consider it my contribution toward Lily's new home. Do you have a certain place you want these when they're ready?" He'd been with her long enough to know she had a plan for every item in her historic home. No detail was too small. She chose each piece of furniture, each knickknack and lamp with care, determined to make her future guests comfortable.

"Yes. Let me show you."

Reid followed her to the wraparound porch, smiling at the bounce in her gait as she moved up the steps.

"I want the rockers along this front section and a few of them on the other side." She moved to the other end where the railing bumped out, widening the area. "One of the swings should go here." She glanced up at the beadboard ceiling. "You may have to get some sturdy hooks to hang it on."

Reid added the items he needed to the materials list on his phone, then peeked in the tall window at the end of the porch. "Is this the tearoom?"

"Would you like to see it?" She pulled a ring of keys from her pocket and opened the door. "I haven't been inside in weeks."

The stillness inside was eerie, the air heavy from lack of fresh air. The only hint of life were the dust motes that floated in the sunlight. A few wooden tables and chairs were scattered around. He noticed Tori's shoulders sag.

"I wanted to bring this back to life. My mom used to bring me here when I was a kid. Sometimes alone, sometimes with my sister, Beth. It was a special mom-and-daughter date."

"It's smaller than I expected."

"It was *the* place to come at one time. Women would gather here and meet friends and talk and drink their tea. The girls offered cookies and petits fours."

"I don't see a kitchen."

"No. They brought everything in from the main one. The door over there opens to the formal dining room. I was so sad when it closed down."

"Why did it?"

"Tastes change. People wanted espresso and flavored coffee in large containers. When the Square Cup coffee shop opened downtown, business here dried up."

He walked to a large shelving unit against the far wall where dozens of teacups were displayed. "That's a lot of teacups."

"They came with the house. I left them there as a reminder. I don't know what I'll do with them. Maybe display them in the main hall with a picture of the old tearoom."

"Or sell them. People might like to take a piece of Camellia Hall history home after their stay here." He scanned the room. "In fact, this would make a great gift shop. You could sell teacups and your fancy jewelry."

"Oh, no, I don't think—"

He watched her eyes soften, then start to sparkle as she thought through the idea. "It wouldn't even take much work, just a good cleaning, more shelving and you'd be good to go."

She wandered around the room, stopping in front of the china shelves. "You know, when I was at the crafters guild the other day, some of the artists were pushing the councilman to build a craft center so the locals could display their goods. What if the gift shop featured local craftsmen?"

"That might generate more income than a tearoom." Her smiled broadened and her energy level started to rise. She was like a beautiful candle coming to life and burning brighter and brighter.

"Yes, and the guests could see firsthand what we have to offer. We'd do everything on consignment." She faced him, and her blue eyes filled with anticipation. "Reid, you have a head for business."

He frowned. "News to me. Undercover work and business aren't on the same planet." Did he have a good business sense? He'd never considered going into business. He'd been too obsessed with justice. There had been a time when he'd thought he'd follow in his dad's footsteps and take over the pharmacy. But now he had no idea what his future would be. He still had a mission to complete for Eddie. Then he'd take some time to sort out the rest of his life.

Right now he was perfectly content to be here working on the old house and helping Tori and Lily.

Content. He couldn't remember the last time he'd experienced that feeling. Maybe it was an indication he was finally distancing himself from his former job? It was a layer of himself he'd gladly shed. This new existence fit him better than he'd expected. Working with his hands was satisfying. Or was working with Tori the reason for the change in his mood?

He needed to get a handle on things because he couldn't afford to get any more entrenched with Tori and his niece. Nothing good could come of it.

Reid made the turn onto Chandler Street late Monday afternoon, admiring the row of mature trees that created a shady canopy over the street. It only added more charm to Tori's already picturesque neighborhood. He'd spent his Saturday working in the yard, trimming shrubs and doing general cleanup. The extra work was welcomed since he still had a rock tumbler of issues rolling around in his head. Sunday he'd spent with Eddie as usual and returned to Dover early this morning to tackle the repair list, which had grown by five items, many of which needed specific supplies. This was his fourth trip to the hardware store. Only this time he came home with something extra.

Reid pulled his truck to a stop at the end of the drive and turned off the engine, his gaze sliding to the passenger seat. He sighed and pinched the bridge of his nose. He doubted his new friend would be welcomed at Camellia Hall. The scruffy dog looked over at him with a canine smile. The mutt was probably grateful for the rescue and looking forward to his new home, but it would depend on whether Tori allowed him to keep the mangy critter or not.

"Come on, Buster. Let's get this over with."

Grabbing hold of the new leash he'd hurriedly purchased, he led the dog out of the truck, bracing himself as the neared the back gate. Buster didn't make the best first impression, but once he was cleaned up he'd be quite presentable. He hoped.

Squeals of delight floated across the lawn as he entered the yard. Lily, dark hair flying, raced toward him, her face bright with joy.

"A dog! You got me a dog!"

Reid stopped in his tracks. Not good. Would Tori think he'd deliberately brought home this critter for Lily? The little girl had mentioned several times how she hoped to have a dog when the inn opened. Before Reid could stop her, Lily stooped down and fiercely hugged the dog's neck. Thankfully, Buster was a perfect gentleman and accepted the affection patiently.

Tori came out onto the back porch, took one

look at the situation and crossed her arms over her chest. “What is that?”

“It’s my dog.” Lily grinned and patted his head.

“Oh, no, it’s not.”

“Aunt Tori, I want to keep him. Please?”

“Out of the question. We’ll get you a nice little dog but not this—” she waved her hand as if searching for words “—thing.”

Reid tugged Buster along with him as he approached his angry employer. “I didn’t plan this. It just happened. The dog was wandering around the parking lot of the hardware store. The owner said he’d been hanging around for several days. He was hungry and lost so I picked him up.”

“If you plan on keeping him, you can’t do it here. A dog like that wouldn’t be good for my business.”

“Well, I guess I could take him to the pound.” He saw her conviction waver. She knew the implications. Buster whined and lay down, looking pitiful. *Good job, fella.*

“Aunt Tori, I love him. Please let him stay.”

He spoke before she could respond. “You know, by the time you open the B and B I’ll be moving on, so Buster won’t be an issue for your guests. Not to mention he’ll be a great watch-dog.” Tori’s glare didn’t fade. “Maybe he could stay with me in the meantime, and Lily could enjoy him until she gets a dog of her own."

He saw the resignation flit across her face and tried not to grin.

"Fine. But you keep him out of the main house and clean him up. He probably has fleas. And for the record, I don't appreciate being manipulated." She spun on her heel and went back inside.

Her parting shot hit him like a laser. He'd been manipulating this situation from the start. It had to stop. Buster glanced up at him. First thing to do was clean up the mutt. "Want to help me give Buster a bath?"

Lily nodded happily. At least one of the women in this house appreciated his new friend.

Tori marched back into the kitchen, added another item to the repair list, then slammed the pen down.

A dog. Reid had brought a dog to the house. A mangy, dirty, flea-ridden critter, and of course Lily had fallen in love with it instantly. Technically, it was Reid's dog, but it was Lily's heart that was involved.

She glanced out the window to see Reid and Lily in the driveway. They'd placed the dog in a galvanized tub and were wetting him down. Surprisingly, the dog didn't seem to mind. Lily was bouncing on her toes happily. She smiled up at Reid and Tori's pulse kicked. Lily liked the handyman, and Tori was becoming concerned. He was a temporary guest, someone passing through their lives for a few weeks. What would happen when Reid moved on? How would it affect Lily?

She moved from the window. He was also her uncle. A blood relative. How would Lily react if she knew? He'd probably be elevated to superhero status, the same honor she'd bestowed on Tori's brothers and brother-in-law.

What would Judy do about the growing attachment to the handyman? Tori rubbed her neck. Probably put an end to it instantly. From here on she'd keep the child away from Reid as much as possible to prevent a strong attachment. She wouldn't show him any special attention, so Lily wouldn't think he was important to her. Even if he was—as a worker, of course. She couldn't forget Reid had an agenda. Letting Lily get too close to Reid was dangerous for both of them. He'd lied once, and he could be lying still for all she knew.

Yet, as much as she hated to admit it, Reid filled her with a sense of hope. She knew he'd do all he could to ensure the repairs were done in time for the opening. Then he'd be moving on, and she could focus on making her new business a success. Her funds would be more than enough to get the bed-and-breakfast off to a good start. Provided she could keep the rooms full and the guests happy.

She glanced out the window again. The doggy bath was over. Buster was shaking off excess water and making Lily giggle. Life was so simple when you were five.

Why was Tori's life so complicated? All she wanted to do was open her business and raise Lily. Instead, she had a shrinking bank account, a house that needed constant attention and now a handyman who was stirring up emotions neither she nor her daughter needed.

She looked up from the kitchen counter when Reid walked in. His T-shirt was damp from bathing the dog. "He's all clean?"

"Pretty much. Lily is going to try to get Buster up onto the glider. She said the swinging would help him dry."

Tori squared her shoulders. She needed to get control right now. And that started with keeping a safe distance between her and Reid. "I know what you're trying to do and I don't appreciate it." His congenial mood faded, and his brows drew together.

"I'm not trying to do anything."

"Oh? You bring this dog here, knowing how

much Lily wants a puppy, and you think you can win her over and then I'll be so grateful that I'll change my mind. Don't think for one moment that appealing to Lily's desire for a dog will cause me to change my mind about your brother."

Reid's dark eyes narrowed. "Not true. I'm not trying to steal her affections. This isn't a contest, so don't make it one. For her sake. I'm not going to kidnap her."

"No, you're not." Tori strode from the room and into her private quarters. She had paperwork to do. She wasn't going to waste another moment on Reid and his not-so-subtle ploys to get her to change her mind.

She didn't speak to him for the rest of the day. To her dismay, the dog followed Lily around and she'd started asking for the critter to be allowed inside. Tori hated to put her foot down since it was obvious her daughter loved the mutt, but she needed to maintain boundaries. She had to admit the dog did look better after a bath, which eased her concern only slightly.

She felt bad about the things she'd said to Reid. She had no real reason to worry he'd take Lily. A man who would rescue a stray dog probably wouldn't kidnap a child. However, the scars Will had left behind were still sensitive. Getting over Reid's subterfuge was going to be hard.

Chapter Seven

Reid stood at the back of the sanctuary Sunday morning, scanning the congregation for Jimmy Ray. He'd invited him to services, and Reid had been eager to accept. Thanks to Eddie, Reid was finding his way back to his faith. In many ways it felt good, but it also cast a glaring light on all his shortcomings. His list of things for which to seek forgiveness was longer than he'd realized.

Spotting the contractor near the front of the church, he started forward. A woman stood and started up the aisle. Tori. He stopped in his tracks. She looked as surprised to see him as he was her. She looked different today in a navy blue dress that ended below her knees. Her hair was hanging around her shoulders in long, soft waves. Normally she wore the golden fawn tresses in a ponytail or clamped together at the back with a big clip. Not today.

"Hello," he said when she reached him.

She nodded, her blue eyes puzzled. "Hi. I didn't expect to see you here."

"It's Sunday. Where else would I be?" He hadn't meant to sound flippant, but this new image of her had him distracted.

"I didn't mean—" She paused. "I didn't know you would be attending my church."

"I've been coming here for the last few weeks. Guess we go to different services. Would you feel better if I went someplace else?" He had no idea why he was baiting her, other than that he enjoyed watching her emotions dance across her face.

She pressed her lips together and tilted her chin upward. "No. You can attend whatever church you please. I was simply surprised. That's all."

He stifled a grin. He really shouldn't be so hard on her. But he knew she'd lumped him into a category that didn't include being a believer.

"Reid, buddy. Good to see you here." Jimmy Ray clapped him on the shoulder, then nodded to Tori. "Morning."

"Hello, Jimmy Ray."

"We have a seat for you up front." He glanced

between him and Tori. "Unless you had plans to sit with Miss Tori."

"No."

She'd spoken so loudly that the people nearby turned to look in her direction. She blushed and rested a hand at her throat. "We were only saying hello. There's no reason to sit together at church. We see each other every day. He lives at my house after all." The woman in the next pew jerked her head up, furrowing her brow at the comment.

"Yes. I do." He was taking delight in her confusion. Her cheeks were a bright shade of pink, and yet she still kept digging.

"In the apartment. Not the house." Finally realizing she'd made things worse, she turned and sat down in the pew. Ignoring him.

Reid grinned inwardly. She was adorable when she was flustered. He was enjoying discovering her various moods. She was endlessly fascinating.

Following his new friend down the aisle, he regretted he couldn't sit with Tori. He'd like to hear her sing the hymns and share prayer time. He puzzled at the unusual desire. He'd never wanted anything so domestic before. Since coming to Dover and working with Tori at the old house, he found himself longing for the ordinary life he'd always scoffed at before.

But he found a certain comfort in eating his meals with Tori and Lily each day.

Still, Eddie had tried that life and failed, and Reid wasn't sure he could set aside his old life for a normal one, either. Would he miss the adrenaline rush when he took down a dealer? Or the palpable tension in his veins when he walked the fine edge of undercover work—allowing himself to be absorbed into the dealer's world, yet keeping a firm hold on his true mission and his dedication to justice?

Could Sundays at church and an eight-to-five job offer anything close?

He glanced over his shoulder at Tori. Maybe. If he had the right person at his side.

The house was quiet when Reid returned with the materials he would need to secure the spindles on the porch and replace the grout in one of the guest bathrooms. The last few days had been filled with a string of repairs that all should have been simple and had, instead, grown more complicated as he worked on them. As a result he'd become a habitual customer at Durrant's Hardware, and he cringed when he thought about the tab he was running up. He felt certain Tori had no idea what he'd been spending on materials and tools.

A scraping sound and a grunt came from

the front of the house. He went to investigate. Tori was attempting to pull a large buffet cabinet across the carpet in the front parlor. "You need some help?"

"Oh, hey. Yes." She brushed loose strands of hair from her face. "I want to move this out into the front hall. It'll make the perfect registration desk. It has plenty of storage, and it's a good height." She grinned and shrugged. "I didn't expect it to be so heavy."

"Let's lift it off the carpet first." Together, they moved the cumbersome piece out into the hallway, positioning it inside the curve of the elegant main staircase.

Tori stepped back and smiled. "Perfect. Thank you. There's one more thing if you don't mind." She led him to the large round table in the corner. "This will fit nicely beside this old settee."

Reid retrieved the item, placing it where Tori indicated. "What will you put in the empty space now?"

"Probably nothing. I'm trying to streamline the furnishings. The rooms are overcrowded and there are too many antiques."

Reid raised his eyebrows. "You buy a historic home to open a bed-and-breakfast and you don't like antiques?"

"Oh, I like them fine, but I want this house

to be like a comfortable home. I don't want my guests to feel they can't sit on the furniture or put their feet up. If they want to have a snack in the back parlor, I want them to feel okay doing so. If people are looking for the high-end antique decor, they can stay at the Lady Banks Inn."

Reid noticed a small cabinet and moved to it. Stroking the top unleashed a rush of long-forgotten memories. "My mom had one like this."

Tori glanced over her shoulder. "Do you still have it?"

"No. I suppose my grandpa sold it. After my parents died there wasn't anyone who wanted the furniture."

"I'm sorry. What happened?"

"They were murdered." Tori's soft gasp settled like a barb in his chest. "My dad was a pharmacist and he owned a store in Slidell, Louisiana. My mom worked there, too. One night as they were closing, a man with a gun broke in looking for drugs. He shot them. Dad died instantly. Mom lived a few days."

"Reid, how horrible. I'm so sorry." She touched his arm. "I can't imagine what you went through."

The sincerity in her tone and the warmth in her touch opened a door deep inside that he'd sealed shut long ago. "Eddie and I went to live with our grandfather after that."

"Did they ever catch the man?"

"Yes. But it didn't change anything."

"No, of course not."

He stepped away. The pity in her eyes soured his stomach. He wasn't sure why he'd confided in her. He never spoke of his parents' deaths. Even he and Eddie never brought it up, as if there was a mutual understanding to leave it buried.

What a stupid move, revealing his past. He didn't want her thinking he was trying to play on her sympathies to get her to agree to take Lily to see her dad. He'd have to be more careful in the future. "So anything else you need moved?"

"Not right now, but I do have a lot of old furniture in the attic to bring downstairs. I'm donating most of it to the flood victims."

"That's very generous of you."

"Not really. It's a way to dispose of things I'll never use anyway."

"You're too modest. You're always thinking of others first." She blushed, and his heart skipped. She had no idea how amazing she was. She caught him staring, and he looked away. "I'm going to get to work on the bathrooms. Call me if you want anything else moved. I don't want you to hurt yourself."

"I will."

He held her gaze and was keenly aware of the sense of connection that vibrated between them again. He didn't understand it. Yes, he was attracted to her, but he'd been attracted to many women in his life. Though none gave him the feeling of belonging the way Tori did. What would she do if he shared that information with her?

He strode down the hall, picked up the bag of materials and took the back stairs to the second floor, not stopping until he was inside the bathroom. He channeled his irritation into digging out the old grout around the tub.

He'd said too much. First he'd bared his soul to Tori about his parents, then he'd paid her a compliment. He couldn't afford to get entangled. He had a mission—to get Lily to her father. He could only do that if he set his emotions completely aside, which was getting harder to do each day.

He pried the last bit of old grout from the edge of the tub and sat back on his heels. The two ladies in this old house burrowed deeper into his heart every day. And he had no idea how to stop it.

* * *

Tori heard Reid's footsteps fade as he went back down the hall. She resisted the urge to watch him, not unlike when she'd run into him at church. He'd looked dashing in a crisp white shirt and dark dress slacks, more polished than his usual jeans and work shirt attire. Her gaze had been drawn to him so frequently she'd barely heard a word the pastor spoke. She had the feeling that other women in the congregation had been looking, too. Reid was a man who turned heads.

Her emotions where he was concerned were a jumbled mess, and she needed time to sort them out. She'd been grateful when he'd come to help her with the buffet. She'd convinced herself she could do it alone, even though she knew it was too cumbersome for her to manage. Reid had appeared at the right moment, stepping in to save the day like he always did. Mr. Helpful. Mr. Handy. Mr. Hero.

Then he'd told her about his parents and everything she thought about him shifted. Murdered. She bit her lip and closed her eyes, the horror of it weighing heavy on her heart. She couldn't begin to image how two young men would deal with such a profound and tragic loss. Reid had apparently funneled his grief into law enforcement, perhaps driven by a need to avenge his parents' deaths. What about his brother? From the little she knew, Eddie must have taken the dark road. A twinge of sympathy formed for Eddie. It must have been hard for a boy to make sense of something so heinous. But he'd had choices, same as Reid.

No. She would not get caught up in finding an excuse for Lily's father. All that mattered was keeping her promise to Judy. Even as she was beginning to question the wisdom of her promise.

An hour later, hunger drove her to the kitchen. The buffet cabinet had proved to be a perfect check-in counter, and she had a dozen ideas on how to utilize the space and make it welcoming.

She glanced up to see Reid walking into the room. "How is the bathroom coming along?"

"Good but I need—"

His cell tone sounded and he slipped it from his pocket and moved off into the hall. She heard him say yes, then he froze. His voice softened and his shoulders hunched as if receiving bad news. When he faced her, the look of sadness in his brown eyes tore at her heart. "What is it?"

"Eddie. My brother. He's had a setback. I need to go."

"How bad is it?" Why was she asking? The

less she knew about the man the better, and the easier to maintain her position. She'd been tempted several times to ask him what exactly was wrong with his brother, but she was afraid if she knew the real circumstances it might influence her, and she didn't need any more conflict in that area.

"At this stage everything is serious."

"I never asked you where he was. Do you have far to go?"

"It's a nursing home in Hammond, Louisiana. It's only a little over an hour from Dover. I'll be back as soon as I can to finish up the bathroom."

He turned to leave, and her conscience prodded her to speak. "Reid. I'll pray for your brother."

He faced her with a sardonic expression. "You'll pray for him, but you won't grant him his dying wish?"

She had no response. Put that way, she was a sorry example of a Christian woman. But she had to think of Judy and the promise she'd made to honor her wishes.

Reid glanced back over his shoulder. "Can you take care of Buster? He's not much trouble. I really can't take him with me."

Great. Not only did she not want the dog, but now she'd have to be responsible for the mutt. She started to refuse, but the look of anxiety in Reid's eyes couldn't be ignored. He was deeply worried for his brother. "Fine. But he's still not coming into the house."

"Thanks."

He walked out the door—and the old house suddenly felt lifeless and empty in a way it never had before.

Lily clasped her little fingers together tightly under her chin, her eyes sorrowful. "*Please* let Buster come inside. He wants to be with me. Mr. Reid always lets Buster inside his house. He was cold and lonely on the back porch last night."

Tori felt herself weakening and had to fight to stand her ground. With Reid away for the last few days seeing to his brother, Buster had become her responsibility. Letting that scruffy, albeit clean and flea-free, animal into the house was out of the question. She was grateful the mutt was well behaved and was surprisingly good with Lily. But what about her forthcoming guests? What if they were allergic to dogs? She couldn't afford to lose business. Thankfully, once Reid was gone, Buster would be, too. She didn't want to think about how Lily would react when that time came.

"No, Lily. He's fine on the porch. You can play with him there. Have you fed him this morning?"

"Yes, ma'am. And I gave him water, too." Lily pouted and went back to the porch, and Tori settled her laptop at the small table in the sunroom so she could keep an eye on her daughter. Should she have given in to make Lily happy? She might have if the request didn't involve other people. Moments like this always made her second-guess her decisions. She tended to be reactionary instead of taking a moment to discuss things with Lily the way Judy had, though, she had to admit, Judy's way rarely worked. Many times Tori had thought things would have gone much better if Lily had had clear rules and boundaries the way she and her brothers and sister had growing up. Mom and Dad had been the ones in charge. Not the children. Period.

She heard Buster bark. Would it be so awful to let the dog in the house? She sighed and chewed her bottom lip. Too many decisions and problems in her head to settle on one. Her gaze drifted to her cell phone. She'd picked it up several times since Reid had left to see how he was and how his brother was doing, but she couldn't make herself call. It wasn't like he was family or anything. He was only a temporary employee.

No, he wasn't. He was a friend. She cared about him, and his loss had touched her deeply. She couldn't imagine how two young boys would deal with having their parents murdered. Maybe letting Lily meet Eddie wasn't such a bad thing. She didn't have to tell her daughter he was her father. Only Reid's brother.

No. She couldn't. All she could do was pray, and she had. Except it had failed to bring peace, instead leaving her feeling like a hypocrite. Reid's last words before he'd left to see Eddie couldn't be ignored. What was the right thing to do?

A short while later Tori glanced up and looked in the yard. She didn't see Lily or the dog. She stood and walked closer to the window. Her heart jumped into her throat when she realized the back gate was open. She hurried out the door, calling for Lily. As she crossed to the driveway she saw Lily and Buster trotting down the drive toward the street, chasing a runaway ball. "Lily, come back here."

"I have to get my ball."

The colorful sphere picked up speed as it hit the slope to the street, and Lily ran faster.

From the corner of her eye Tori saw a car coming down the street. She broke into a run. "Lily. Stop!"

She knew she'd never make it in time. "Lord, please save her."

Buster loped in front of Lily with a loud bark, causing the girl to fall down onto the drive, landing on her behind. Tori blinked, then raced forward, scooping the little girl into her arms. "Lily, don't ever do that again. You could have been seriously hurt."

Lily teared up. "Buster knocked me down."

Tori glanced at the dog, who stared back at her with expectation. "Buster. You are my hero. Thank you. I take back every bad thing I ever said about you. Come on, Lily. Let's get back into the yard. I'll get your ball later."

With Lily and the dog safely in the backyard and the ball retrieved, Tori sat on the glider swing, reflecting on the terrifying event. It was strange the way things worked out. She'd been wrong about Buster. He had protected her daughter, instinctively getting between her and the oncoming car. If Reid hadn't brought the dog home, Lily might have been in the path of that vehicle.

If Reid hadn't shown up, she wouldn't be this close to getting the B and B open. She'd changed her mind about Reid. And now

Buster. Should she change her mind about Lily's father, too? How would she live with herself if she went against Judy's wishes? But how would she deal with Lily when she asked about her father? How could she explain that she could have met him, but Tori had refused to allow it? Lily wouldn't be upset with Judy. She'd be angry at her.

There was no simple answer. She had to focus on the present. The inspector was coming in the morning. That's all she should be thinking about right now.

Reid stared out the window of his brother's room at the small pond with the fountain in the center. It was surrounded by a grove of live oaks decorated with lacy Spanish moss, creating a soothing vista that calmed the spirit. Eddie had commented on it many times since coming here. He only wished his brother was strong enough to stroll around the lovely grounds, but it was out of the question now. He doubted even a ride in a wheelchair would be possible. His recent setback had cost him time he couldn't afford.

"Hey, bro."

Reid moved back to the bed. Eddie was smiling up at him, albeit feebly. But the lift in his spirits was welcome. "Hey. 'Bout time you woke up. This place has turned you into a lazy bum." He took his brother's hand and squeezed it. "You gave me quite a scare."

"Scared myself. I was afraid it was the final hour, and I would never get to see my little girl."

"I'm working on it, Eddie. I promise, but Tori is devoted to Judy and she sees her promise to never acknowledge you as sacred. She believes if she lets Lily meet you, she would be betraying her friend's dying wish."

"What about my dying wish?"

Reid's heart burned. "I know."

"This latest relapse of mine has got me to thinking. I want you to set things up for Lily to get whatever inheritance I have from Mom and Dad. I know you've kept those funds over the years. Maybe my portion will allow Lily to go to college or help Tori with the bed-and-breakfast. Talk to Tori, convince her the money is for Lily because I love her, not out of some attempt to buy her forgiveness or get her to come here."

Tears stung the backs of his eyes. "I will. Don't worry, I'll set it all up."

"Thanks. If I never get to see Lily, at least I'll know I provided for her future in some small way."

"You're a good man, Edward Blackthorn."

"No. Just a sinner saved by grace. I wish I'd found the Lord sooner. He'd been trying to get my attention ever since I walked out on Judy, but I didn't want to hear him. Won't be long till I'll be able to talk to him face-to-face. What a moment, huh?"

"Not for a while, little brother. We have things to do. I'm not ready to let you go so soon."

"Then I'll do my best to hang on as long as possible."

Exhausted, Eddie closed his eyes and drifted off. Reid's chest squeezed so tight he could barely breathe. He had to concentrate on making the most of every moment, and he'd start with renewing his efforts to get Tori to change her mind.

Tori's nerves were on edge from the moment she woke up the next day in anticipation of the inspector's visit. When he'd finally shown up she'd retreated to the sunroom, but found sitting still impossible. Instead, she wandered the hallway, trying to look busy and attempting to read the man's expression as he moved about the house.

To her dismay, she found herself wishing Reid was here. His absence had been keenly felt. At least a dozen times during the day she found herself wanting to ask him a question or seek his help. Everything seemed more difficult without him. He always made her feel strong and confident. She hated that. She was an independent woman capable of handling her own life, but Reid's belief in her dream, his support, gave her extra confidence during these stressful final weeks before opening. Mostly she wished he was here to hold her hand through this inspection.

He'd sent a text to let her know Eddie was stabilized and that he'd be back to work on Monday. He'd even wished her good luck with the inspection. It would be too easy to start relying on him for more than repair work. She looked forward to the evening mealtime when they would discuss the day's accomplishments and listen to Lily's chatter about her day. She warned herself to regain the distance she had kept at the beginning, but it was becoming harder to do.

Reid was a fascinating man. Smart, kind, and his gentleness toward Lily touched her heart. She had to admit, having someone to share the load had eased much of her stress. He'd changed since he'd been at Camellia Hall. The cool, aloof demeanor had softened. He was approachable and relaxed, though his presence still did outlandish things to her nervous system.

She appreciated him sticking to their deal. He hadn't pressed her once about going to see Lily's father. But she had to admit she was beginning to question Judy's choice to deny Eddie's existence. The man was dying after all. Did she have a right to keep Lily from seeing her only living parent, no matter what he'd done?

The inspector strode past in the center hallway. He'd been upstairs looking at plumbing and roofing. She opened her mouth to ask how it was going, but changed her mind.

She had confidence in her contractor's work and the guidance of her restoration specialist, so she felt certain those things would pass, but she'd also been told by a few owners of other historic properties in town that the process often found unexpected issues that had to be addressed before the funds could be released. More issues meant another waiting period, and she couldn't afford more delays. She had to pass today.

A half hour later the inspector stepped into the front parlor, where she was arranging a cozy conversation area.

"I'll be going now. You should receive a report in the mail in a few days."

Tori watched with a heavy heart as the slender, balding older man walked out. He hadn't smiled, hadn't offered an encouraging word. Her stomach sank. It was going to be a long couple of days.

By Sunday she'd worried herself into a frazzle over the inspection report. Tori pulled her thoughts away from her troubles and back to the sermon Reverend Barrett was delivering. Maybe she should have stayed home this morning. She'd been tired and anxious since the inspection, vacillating between confidence that she'd pass with flying colors and dread she would fail and not get the funds she so desperately needed.

"Compassion. It's the first trait the Lord mentions about himself. Then he must hold that quality in highest regard."

The pastor's words grabbed her full attention.

"Yet oftentimes we find it hard to show compassion to others. Our tendency is to judge others to see if they deserve our compassion. We tell ourselves they got what they deserved, or we decide their behavior or situation is too egregious to sympathize with. It's easy to show compassion to the person battling cancer, or the grieving family. But what about showing compassion to those who have hurt us or betrayed us? The Lord displayed compassion to everyone, no matter their station or situation. Should we do any less?"

His words reverberated in her mind long after a quiet afternoon with Lily at Friendship Park and Sunday dinner with her family. She was withholding compassion from Lily's father out of devotion to Judy. It also stemmed from her own sense of anger and resentment at his treatment of her friend. But didn't the man deserve compassion for the life he'd led that was now costing him an early death?

Lord, how do I do that? I can't get past the wreckage he left behind.

After tucking Lily in bed that night, she curled up on the sofa and reached for the remote. She wanted to escape, and the movie she'd recorded yesterday was exactly what she needed. As it filled the screen, her cell rang.

Tori frowned at the name on the display. Why would Councilman Holmes be calling her, and on a Sunday evening? *Please don't let it be more issues with the house.*

"Hello Tori. This is Dick Holmes."

"Yes, sir, what can I do for you?"

"I wanted to give you a heads-up on something. Seems a few of your neighbors aren't too happy about having a business next door.

They've filed a complaint. They're trying to say you're violating zoning laws by having a bed-and-breakfast in a residential area."

"That's absurd. We have approval from the zoning board, and a B and B is by nature in a residential area. That's the point."

"I know. I explained all that to them, and they're still not happy. They plan on confronting you personally about this."

Would the problems ever stop coming? "Can you tell me who they are?"

Dick mentioned four names that Tori recognized. The street was lined with some of the oldest homes in Dover, families who had been there for generations, and she knew three of the women through her church and various community projects. The fourth was new to the neighborhood, having moved into one of the old homes shortly after Tori bought Camellia Hall. She had children a few years older than Lily. They'd only met once, but she'd seemed nice.

"Thank you, Dick. I'll be ready when they come by." She couldn't imagine why the women had suddenly banded together to complain. She knew some neighbors had been upset that the construction had gone on too long, and the trucks parked in the street had been an eyesore. But there'd been no complaints lately. Why the sudden change of heart?

She wanted to cry. She wanted to talk to Reid. He always had a solution for her problems. There she went again, looking to someone else for help. She would handle this on her own.

So why did that thought make her feel so sad?

Reid pulled the truck into the driveway and applied the brakes. His heart softened as he looked at the ornate old home that was Camellia Hall. When a sense of coming home settled around his shoulders, he quickly shook it off. This wasn't his home and never would be, but for the time being he would allow himself to enjoy the warmth and welcome.

He parked at the garage and hopped out of the truck, the anticipation at seeing Tori and Lily quickening his blood. He'd been tempted to call her, especially on the day of the inspection, but he'd decided against it. Time apart might be the best course of action right now. They both had deep, emotional reasons to hold their ground. He prayed somehow the Lord would move them to a place where they could agree and Eddie would get to see his little girl.

Stepping through the back gate, he looked

around for Buster, who usually launched himself at him the moment he arrived. A pinch of fear touched his mind. Had Tori taken the opportunity of his absence during the past few days to get rid of the dog?

He tapped on the back door before entering, then called for Tori, uncertain of the kind of reception he'd receive. "Anybody here?" Buster rounded the corner with a loud bark and charged toward him. He knelt down to give the lovable mutt some scratches behind his floppy ears. "What are you doing inside, fella? You're not allowed in here. You're going to be in big trouble."

"Not anymore."

Reid looked up into Tori's blue eyes, and the sparkle in them landed inside his heart. He stood, struggling to find his breath. How was it possible that she became more beautiful each time he saw her? "You changed your mind?"

She grinned and shrugged her shoulders. "I had no choice. He saved Lily's life. He deserves to live in the house now."

"What? Is Lily okay? What happened?"

"He threw himself in front of her to keep her from running into the path of an oncoming car."

Reid's heart stopped beating. The thought

of little Lily in that situation chilled his blood. He ran a hand down his jaw. "Thank God."

"I figured he needed a second chance. He is a hero after all."

Her words pierced him. "So does that apply to everyone?"

"What do you mean?"

"Buster proved his worth. What about Eddie? Doesn't he deserve a second chance, too?"

Tori's smile vanished. "We agreed not to discuss that."

Her posture told him not to pursue the issue, but he wasn't giving up.

She raised her chin, her blue eyes shaded. "How is your brother?"

"Stabilized. But the doctors said it could be something else tomorrow. His body is slowly shutting down."

"I'm sorry. I know what it's like to see someone you love slowly slip away."

"Yes, you do." Reid saw a small glimmer of hope. Maybe if Tori could recall her feelings as Judy faded away, she could find some compassion in her heart for Eddie. "How did the inspection go? I wish I could've been here."

She shrugged. "Okay, I guess. He didn't say a word, just wandered all over the house with a tablet making notes. He said I should have a report in a few days. I'm hoping it'll come tomorrow. I really need those funds."

Maybe now was the time to present Eddie's request. "I may have an answer for you that could help, especially if the funds are delayed."

She met his eyes, and his hope rose. He'd like nothing more than to ease her anxiety and let her finish her dream. He took a moment to organize his words. "When our parents died, the estate was left to us, but after our grandfather passed I became the executor. Eddie never touched his inheritance, and he told me he'd like to leave it to Lily. It's a considerable sum, Tori, enough for her college and to finish the B and B."

Tori's eyes darkened to navy blue. Her mouth set in a hard line. "Now he wants to bribe me into bringing Lily to see him? He thinks giving me money will absolve him of his guilt? There's not enough money in the world to make up for what he did to Judy. He doesn't deserve to see her. Ever." She crossed her arms over her chest. "I should have expected something like this. Well, I can't be bought, and neither can Lily, so you can go back to your no-account brother and tell him no thank you."

"What happened to second chances, Tori?

You'll give me and the dog a new chance, but not my brother, who's dying?"

"If it were up to me I might consider it, but it's not. It's what Judy wanted, and I intend to honor her dying wish."

"And I'm equally committed to granting my brother's dying wish. So we're not very different in our intent, are we?"

"It's not the same thing at all. I can't let her down. I've let too many people down in my life, and this time I'm standing my ground."

Reid sat on a kitchen stool, clasping his hands together on the granite countertop. He doubted his next words would make any difference, but he felt compelled to say them. "It's my fault Eddie is dying."

"What do you mean?"

"He came to me for money right after I became executor of the estate. I was in the service and Eddie was still at home. Gramps had told me he'd gotten in with a bad crowd and was doing drugs. I told Eddie I wasn't going to release any of his inheritance until he got clean. I knew he'd just blow it all on drugs and booze. He was furious. I figured Eddie would get his life together and call me."

"He didn't?"

"I don't know. We didn't speak for the next six years."

"Why?"

"I was focused on getting justice. At least that's what I told myself. I wanted to take down as many drug dealers as I could. I didn't think about my brother much." He sighed and set his jaw. "The point is, I promised my mom I'd look after him. He was a sweet kid and he'd looked up to me. But when he needed me I turned away. If I'd thought about him more from the beginning, I might have been able to keep him clear of that lifestyle. But I wasn't there. I was out chasing my own goals."

"Don't you mean demons?"

"Maybe."

Tori slid onto the stool beside him. A light, sweet fragrance curled around him.

"I know a little about that. When my dad died suddenly, the family was thrown into chaos. We each had to deal with it in our own way. My way was to run. Being around the house, not having him there, not talking to him every day was so hard. Sometimes I couldn't breathe, the loss was so painful. The only way I could cope was to leave town. That's when I went to stay with Judy. It wasn't long after that that she was diagnosed, and helping her and Lily became my focus. Dad always told me I was destined to do something wonderful. He believed in me. But I never could find the one thing I was good at or loved. My brothers and sister always knew what they wanted to be. I always felt like I'd failed to live up to his expectations. I hated letting him down."

"I don't think you have. Deciding to raise Lily is a wonderful thing. I think it's pretty awesome."

"Thank you, but what if I mess it up? What if I get tired of being her mom the way I did with my other projects?"

"You already know the answer to that, I think." He resisted the impulse to take her hand.

"I suppose. She's so incredible. Each day she changes."

"I can remember my mom telling us when she was frustrated with something we'd done that she was making it up as she went along. She wished she'd had a guidebook."

"My sisters tell me the same thing. They keep saying I'm worrying too much."

"I guess we're both struggling with guilt."

She smiled and nodded. "So what do we do?"

"Remind each other to go easy on ourselves."

"And each other?"

"I'd like that."

"I'll try but I can't promise anything. Yet."

Reid watched her leave, a swell of encouragement settling in his mind.

Yet. One little word that held a universe of hope.

"And thank You, Jesus, for bringing Mr. Reid back to our house. I love him. Amen."

Tori pulled the covers over her daughter and kissed her forehead. "Sleep tight. I love you."

"I love you more. Aren't you glad Mr. Reid is back? He's really good at fixin' things, isn't he?"

"Yes, he is. Why do you like him so much?"

Lily's eyes brightened, and she sat up. "'Cause he's big and strong and he reads good and he makes me feel all fuzzy inside."

"What do you mean?"

"He's like when I hug my teddy bear. I get all squishy 'cause he's so warm and soft and cuddly."

Cuddly wasn't a word she would ever use to describe Reid. He was all muscle and strength and hard edges. Though she couldn't argue with the *strong* and *good reader* parts.

Curled up on the sofa later, she hugged a pillow to her chest and tried to sort out her thoughts. She and Reid had reached a point of common ground today. They both felt guilty about failures in their pasts. She'd never thought of Reid carrying a load of guilt. He'd always behaved like he could handle anything. Strangely enough, knowing he felt regret made him more attractive. More human. And that was not good. She was already attracted to him. She didn't need any more sterling qualities to draw her closer. Then she'd have to seriously consider his request, which meant being disloyal to her friend.

If only Reid had stayed the mysterious, detached man who had appeared in her sunroom and rescued her from her own stupidity. But he wasn't. Every day he burrowed deeper into their lives and the community. He did so much for others, and he'd become more involved in the flood home project. Last week he and Jimmy Ray had rented a moving van and gone around town gathering the donated furniture and taking them to one of the warehouses at Montgomery Electrical. Her brothers had offered the space as a collection point for all the items that would eventually occupy the flood houses. He'd hauled off most of the things in her attic.

A warm spot of compassion had formed in her chest after she and Reid had confessed their failures and guilt. His desire to grant his brother's dying wish went deeper than family obligation. He was trying to make up for the past, the same way she was.

A noise on the front porch sent a jolt of adrenaline through her veins. The mailman. According to her calculations, the report from the inspection should arrive today. The box beside the front door was stuffed full as she gathered up the envelopes. She needed to get a post-office box for all her business mail. Another item on her list she hadn't gotten around to yet. She sorted through the mail, inhaling a sharp breath at the return address on the largest one. Mississippi State Preservation Commission.

The envelope opened easily and she scanned the enclosed report, her heart racing, only to stop beating at the last paragraph. Everything looked good, but there was one thing the inspector hadn't seen, which forced him to fail the inspection. No handicap ramp leading up to the porch.

"No. That's wrong." There had to be a mistake. She'd been told she didn't need a ramp. She had the papers to prove it somewhere. She sank onto the old settee in the hallway, fighting tears. She needed her reimbursement funds released so she could open on time.

Maybe it was time to face reality? Had she bitten off more than she could chew? Was her family right—was running a bed-and-breakfast alone too big a job? Should she call the whole thing off, sell out and get a regular job? Her mind rejected the notion, but the obstacles felt insurmountable.

She stood and took the main staircase to the attic, then the few steps leading to the windowed tower. Leaning against the frame, she stared out at the sprawling landscape. She could see downtown from here, the church steeple, the courthouse dome. It had become her favorite spot for thinking and sorting out her roller-coaster emotions during the project. The small lookout symbolically lifted her above the fray and the problems downstairs, and gave her a fresh perspective and a quiet place to pray. At the moment, even praying was too hard.

With her head against the windowpane, she closed her eyes as the tears began to fall.

Chapter Eight

Reid spotted Tori up in the tower as he turned into the driveway. In the short time he'd been working for her, he'd learned it was her go-to place when she needed to sort out things. He could only imagine the amount of stress on her slender shoulders as she worked to get this business running. But today there was something odd about her presence in the tower. It looked like she had her forehead against the glass, as if she were defeated. Not good. He'd made it his goal to make sure nothing got her down.

He saw the stack of mail on the settee as he walked past. One envelope had been opened, and the letter lay unfolded beside it. From the return address, he knew it must be the inspection report. He was tempted to read it but decided not to. She would tell him if she wanted to, though the fact that she had taken to the tower didn't bode well.

He made his way as quietly as possible to the attic and the tower. Her shoulders were shaking and he could hear muffled sobs. "Tori."

She stiffened and wiped her face, keeping her back to him. Trying to hide her emotions, it seemed.

"I saw the envelope from the commission."

"Did you read the letter?"

"No."

"I failed." She wiped her eyes before facing him. "He said I didn't have a handicap ramp, but I'm not required to. If you only have five guest rooms then you don't need one. This is a historic home, one of only six Steamboat Gothics in the country. Putting a ramp on this house would destroy the historic integrity. That's not me saying that, it's the National Register, the Americans with Disabilities Act and the local preservation society. It was all settled when I bought the house. But now this local guy is insisting I have one put in before he'll agree to release my funds. I can't afford to do that, and it'll take too much time."

She ran her a palm over her cheek as fresh tears rolled down, and it was all he could do to keep from pulling her into his arms.

"And now the neighbors are in an uproar about my opening a bed-and-breakfast in the neighborhood. But that was settled, too. I'm not breaking any zoning laws."

Her blue eyes were sad and pleading as she looked at him. "What am I going to do?"

Her vulnerability was too much to handle. He'd never been good at dealing with emotions, but seeing Tori like this compelled him to reach out and pull her into his embrace. She didn't resist. He held her, marveling at how right she felt in his arms, cradled against his heart.

"We'll work it out. Have you called your attorney?"

She shook her head, releasing a waft of strawberry scent from her hair. "But I intend to. I'm going to call everyone in the entire state if I have to."

He smiled and held her a bit closer. "That's my girl." Tori wouldn't simply accept this setback. "Get your people working on this, and we'll get back to work making the place shine."

"But I can't stand around and do nothing."

She looked up at him with her tearstained cheeks and blue eyes filled with worry, and he knew he had to do something to ease her distress. "How about this? Let me do some research and take some measurements and see what I can come up with to build a ramp."

"But the cost—"

"Shh. Add it to my tab. We'll settle up later."

"I don't know. There's still the matter of the time involved. And getting approval. Even if we build a ramp, we can't start on it until it's OK'd and we get a permit."

"Tell your people what we're doing and see if they can grease the wheels. In the meantime, I'll look into the construction end."

She nodded, then looked up at him.

The air between them crackled. The bond that had sparked between them the first day flared to life. He knew she felt it, too. Her gaze lingered on his mouth, and he wanted nothing more at this moment than to pull her closer and kiss those lips that had tempted him from the first moment he'd seen her.

Common sense arrived. This was not the time to cross any barriers, and kissing her now would be taking advantage of her emotional state. They'd reached common ground, and he didn't want to mess that up. He placed a light kiss on her forehead and stepped back. "Come on. Let's get busy. Maybe we can avert this before it gets too far down the pike."

She preceded him out and into the vast attic.

"Maybe I can talk to the neighbors and ease some of their fears. Reach out to them first."

"Good idea. A preemptive strike." He took her arm. "You'll get through this. You're a fighter. You'll win the battle."

"Thanks." Her smile beamed like a ray of sunlight, piercing the gloomy attic and sending his heart pounding. He found himself wondering what might have happened between them if the shadows of Eddie and Judy weren't looming overhead.

At the bottom of the attic stairs, Reid closed the door and faced her. "Feeling better?"

"Yes. I think I know how to approach the neighbors. But first I have to pick up Lily. And I'll see what I can come up with to satisfy the inspector about the ramp in case you have to follow through on that."

Reid watched her walk away, his mind troubled. Every day he could feel his emotional roots burrowing deeper into the lives of Tori and Lily. His comfort level eased each morning when he woke and realized he was settling into small-town life.

But was he suitable for this kind of life? Was he deserving? Could he set aside the last several years and become a normal, family-oriented man? His heart wanted that, but his practical brain had serious doubts. There were things he'd done undercover that Tori could never know. Which meant he'd be keeping secrets again, the one thing she hated.

He'd be smart to keep his emotions intact. Approach the rest of his time here as another undercover operation. Stay focused on the task, keep emotions locked up and accomplish the mission.

For the first time, he found he didn't want to live that way.

Tori pulled the cinnamon muffins from the oven Friday morning, gingerly plucking them from the pan and placing them in the silver weave basket. The sweet aroma boosted her confidence. The house would smell warm and welcoming when the ladies arrived.

She'd planned it all out on her way to pick up Lily the day the letter had arrived. First she had sent each woman a personal invitation on her new Camellia Hall stationery. Next came the menu. She would brew up a pot of the Smiley girls' famous mint tea, bake the muffins, then give the women a tour of the house and outline her business plan to alleviate their concerns. She wasn't too concerned about Virginia Bower, Janet Craig or Diane Fogle. They were probably not too upset. She suspected Naomi Foster was the instigator of the complaint, since she was new to Dover and probably unfamiliar with how things worked.

She carried the muffins into the front parlor, where she'd set up a table surrounded by comfy but elegant antique chairs. She wanted this to be a friendly, relaxed meeting. She'd made a small nosegay-style arrangement of pink and yellow roses from the yard in a silver mint julep cup. A glance at the grandfather clock near the door sent a surge of excitement along her veins. They should be here any moment.

As if on cue, the doorbell rang. Showtime. Offering up a prayer, she opened the door, smiling warmly. "Welcome to Camellia Hall."

From the look on the women's faces, she had her work cut out for her. She turned her smile up a notch and ushered the ladies inside.

Tori pulled another slice of pizza from the box that evening, hoping one more piece would infuse her with some energy. Dealing with the neighbors had left her drained and exhausted. She'd been relieved when they'd left. By the time she'd cleaned up, picked up Lily from school and run a few errands, she'd been too tired to think about fixing an evening meal. Reid had come to her rescue when he'd appeared at the house with a box of hot, mouthwatering pizza.

His thoughtfulness had touched her, and she'd suggested they eat in the private quarters instead of the breakfast room in the main house as they usually did. Tonight she needed the comfort of her own space, and Reid had earned the right to join them.

Several times he'd passed through the house while her guests were there, and he'd given her a thumbs-up. It had encouraged her and lifted her spirits each time. All in all, she felt the visit had gone well. She'd answered all their questions and eased their concerns about having a business in the neighborhood. She'd reassured them there would be no loud gatherings since it wouldn't be a party venue, and pointed out that the guests would be gone during the day and only in the house at night to sleep. She pointed out how the parking area beside the garage was more than adequate to hold the guests' vehicles, even when the inn was full.

But she was convinced it had been the tour of the old house that had won them over. They'd been surprised at how homey and comfortable the rooms were. Her confidence had been soaring as the women left. Diane had hung back, telling her she suspected Naomi had been reassured and would most likely withdraw her complaint.

"Have you heard back from the complaint committee?" Reid took a sip of his cola and reached for another slice of pizza.

Tori pulled her attention back to the sketches he'd done for the proposed ramp. "Not yet, but I have a good feeling about it."

"So do I. You did a great job of charming them."

"How do you know that?"

"I saw their faces. Your passion and enthusiasm are contagious. How could they not catch the excitement and change their minds?"

Her cheeks warmed at his sincere compliment. "I only wanted to make them understand and ease their concerns."

"You did. Big-time."

"Thanks." She tapped the drawings. "Speaking of concerns, this ramp is perfect. It'll satisfy the commission, but it won't intrude on the integrity of the house."

"It'll be a bit more expensive to build, but it should make everyone happy."

She sighed and ran a hand through the hair at her temple. "I hope so. I'll take it to them tomorrow. My attorney has convinced those involved to make a decision in the next couple of days. I just can't afford to waste any time.

Every time I look at the calendar, I get a knot in my chest."

"You'll make it. The repair list gets smaller every day."

"I know you're working hard to get it all done. Thank you. I couldn't have done this without you."

"Sure you could."

Tori glanced at the plans again. "How long will it take to build this ramp?"

"A day."

"Really? Good. I might hear from the commission in the next day or two. So you could start soon."

"As soon as we get the go-ahead."

Reid's cell sounded, and after a quick glance he excused himself and moved across the room. "Hey, Phil. What's up?"

Tori noticed Reid's shoulders stiffen as he spoke on the phone, and her curiosity spiked. Bad news about his brother, perhaps?

"Okay. I'll be there."

When he returned to the table, his expression was dark and troubled. "Reid, what's wrong?"

He eased into the chair, his jaw flexing. "I have to leave town."

"What? Why?"

"That was my old boss. My last case is finally coming to court. I need to go to Dallas next week to testify."

"How long will you be gone?" Time was precious. She couldn't afford any delays.

"A few days, I think. But there's no way of knowing for sure."

Her gaze dropped to the ramp sketches. How was she going to get everything done without Reid?

He reached over and squeezed her hand. "I'll get back as soon as possible. Promise. We'll get the ramp done."

"I know." She knew he'd do everything he could, but she still worried.

Reid glanced over at the sofa where Lily and Buster were fast asleep. "Looks like our little girl has had enough for today."

Our little girl. Is that how he thought of them, as a family? Best not to follow that line of thought. "Too much fun and too much pizza." Tori stood. "I'd better get her to bed."

"I'll carry her." Without waiting for a reply, he scooped the little child into his arms, holding her securely against his chest.

He laid Lily gently on the bed, and Tori fought the image forming in her mind of mother and father putting their little girl to bed. She tucked the sleeping girl in, placing a kiss on her sweet cheek, then looked up to find Reid staring at her. His coffee-colored eyes were soft and filled with a warm light. Her heart floated in her chest. He looked at her as if he cared.

Could he see into her heart? She wanted him to. Which was clearly a big mistake. When he finally looked away, his gaze landed on the sleeping Lily, his expression one of complete love. He loved his niece. She had no doubt. And Lily adored him. Did she have a right to keep them apart?

She'd accused Reid of lying for not telling her the whole truth from the first. But she was doing the same thing—sharing only part of the truth.

They really had more in common than she wanted to admit. Tori came around the bed and stopped at his side, looking lovingly at her daughter. She rested her hand on his arm. "She's so beautiful when she's asleep."

"And quiet."

Tori nodded with a smile. "She does like to talk." They made their way silently back downstairs.

"I didn't know five-year-olds knew that many words. Or had so much imagination."

"You mean like dressing Buster up with a feather boa and a hat?"

"I have to admit I wasn't expecting that

when I brought the pizza inside. He looked pretty funny, though I don't think he appreciated the outfit."

He caught her gaze and smiled. Her breath caught. His smile stole the starch from her knees. It was wide and warm and utterly charming. There was a small crease on one side of his mouth that was completely adorable. She couldn't look away. In all the weeks she'd known him, he had never smiled. A faint grin maybe, but never a full-on smile.

"Is everything all right?"

She nodded, smiling. "You should do that more often."

"What?"

"Smile."

He drew his finger across his chin, as if embarrassed. "I haven't had much reason to smile the last few years."

"Well, it's quite a sight."

"You think so?"

"I do."

"Then I'll try to find more reasons to display it."

Tori looked into his eyes and saw a warmth and lightness she'd never seen before. Was it possible that being here with her and Lily had softened his hard edges? The notion boosted her spirits.

Reid rested his hand on the side of her face. "You are one of the biggest incentives. You make everyone around you want to smile."

Suddenly he lowered his hand and stepped back. "I'd better go. Lots to do tomorrow."

Dazed, she nodded and hurried to regroup. "Thanks for the pizza. That was nice."

"I thought it was about time I gave you a break from feeding me."

"I don't mind. You're easy to cook for. You'll eat anything."

He didn't smile, only hurried out the door. Had he guessed her feelings toward him and was running for the hills? She couldn't help recalling that first moment when they'd looked into each other's eyes and she felt a connection—a link she'd never experienced before. She'd thought then that he could see straight through to her heart.

Maybe he actually could. And, if so, she'd better keep her emotions in check.

Reid slid behind the wheel of his truck Saturday morning at the crack of dawn. He was headed to meet up with Jimmy Ray at the Montgomery warehouse with the other volunteers for the flood house project. The early hour suited him since he hadn't slept much last night. Putting Lily to bed had cracked open something deep inside, and he wasn't sure what to do with the emotions. He'd watched in fascination as Tori had tucked her in and kissed her forehead. He'd had the oddest desire to do the same. A swell of overpowering love lodged in his throat, along with a fierce desire to protect this precious life at any cost.

Is this what being a father felt like?

He'd been unable to take his gaze from the look of complete love and devotion on Tori's face. Her love for Lily shone like a light from within. She was an intriguing woman. He liked being part of her life here at the hall. What would it be like to stay and work side by side with her?

His fingers twitched as he recalled the silky feel of her skin under his palm when he'd touched her cheek last night.

The thought of testifying in court intruded on his mind, killing the tender emotions. All this domesticity at Camellia Hall was giving him ideas he shouldn't entertain. Yet he was reluctant to return to the hard-edged world of law enforcement. Testifying would dredge up all the things he'd hoped to put behind him when he quit.

But he had Tori and Lily and Camellia Hall to come back to. The idea filled him with more peace and joy than he'd known since he'd been a kid and his parents had been alive. But the big question still loomed: Was he capable of such a drastic change?

Reid had never seen anything like the turnout at the Montgomery Electrical warehouse. Volunteers by the dozens had come together to fill six vans, one for each flooded home, with everything they would need to start over. From furniture to salt and pepper shakers, nothing had been overlooked.

The Montgomerys were providing not only the space to store all the donated items, but the vehicles to deliver them. He'd arrived early to help divide and load furniture into the back of each van. Now he was packing the small appliances for each family into a large carton, but his gaze was on Tori as she worked alongside her family. He'd met them all today, the brothers and their wives and children. Her sister, Bethany, expecting her first child, and Francie, the matriarch, who beamed with pride as she worked alongside her children. Even the grandkids were helping out. The ones old enough were writing labels on boxes and packing light items. The smaller children, including Lily, were being entertained in the main office.

Tori's family was an interesting bunch.

Warm, friendly and eager to help. They reminded him of his family when they had volunteered for various projects at church or in the community. He'd forgotten about those times. Eddie, despite his Swiss cheese memory, frequently nudged him to remember the happy times and not the way it had all ended.

But the end is what had defined his adult life. The pain, the loss, the horror of it had been his driving force, justice his only goal. Now he wanted more. He wanted that normal family life again. Quiet evenings on the front porch and Sunday dinners at the in-laws.

His gaze sought Tori, as it had every few minutes since she'd arrived. She was working with one of her sisters-in-law, Julie, if he remembered correctly, sorting through the mountain of clothing for the proper size for each family member. She glowed. She was born to help others, to make them feel welcome. She would be a phenomenal hostess for the bed-and-breakfast, and she was a wonderful mother to Lily. He wished he could make her see that. She still felt as if she would fail her daughter, and her efforts to be the mother her friend would have been was only putting stress on her that she didn't need. She simply needed to trust her instincts.

The sound of her unmistakable laughter

drew his gaze to her again. His heart skipped a beat at the sight of her generous smile. Happiness made her sparkle. As if sensing his scrutiny, she caught his gaze. He grinned and nodded. Every other woman in the place faded into the background. He'd never known a woman like her. She was stressed to the max about getting her B and B open on time despite the unexpected obstacles that had cropped up, but she still found time to collect and organize the items for the victims. She was amazing. Too amazing for a man like him.

A warmth spread across his chest as he placed the last item in the box. He'd spent much of his free time working on the homes and seeing them all to completion. Nothing had given him this kind of satisfaction before. Helping clean and rebuild the flood houses had restored his faith in people and in the Lord's grace. The generosity of this small town never ceased to amaze him, and it increased his desire to stay.

But he only wanted to stay if Tori and Lily were part of the picture, and he didn't see that happening.

Sealing up the carton, Reid wrote the name of the family on the top before carrying it outside and stowing it in the back of the nearly full van. Two of the trucks had already left to deliver their goods. Other volunteers would be waiting to unload, place the furnishings and put away the household goods. By the end of the day, all six families would have everything they needed to reclaim their lives.

Reid spotted the man as he headed back inside the warehouse. He stood at the edge of the parking lot, leaning against the back of a Montgomery company truck. At first he assumed it was one of the regular employees, but something about the arrogant stance drew a closer look. His heart chilled.

Archer.

What was he doing here? How had he found him? No one but his old boss knew where he'd gone after his last case. He took a step toward the man, but a pickup pulled into the parking lot, blocking his way. When he looked again the man was gone. But it was Archer. He was positive.

Fury sent his blood roaring in his ears. He had to find out why Archer was loose and get him out of Dover. He hadn't anticipated his past threatening his future. He had no idea how Archer had learned his real name. Safeguards were in place to prevent this very thing.

A quick call to his old boss revealed Archer had been released on a technicality, but the authorities had a new arrest warrant for another crime. At least now he had a good reason to apprehend the man next time he showed up.

Inside the warehouse, Reid scanned the area for Seth Montgomery. They'd bonded quickly over their similar professions, and he was going to need his help. If Archer showed up again, he'd be prepared with backup.

Chapter Nine

The soft veil of fall twilight settled over Camellia Hall. The days were getting shorter, and the pending time change would shorten the days even further, bringing darkness before the evening meal.

Tori let the rhythmic to-and-fro of the old glider ease her fatigue. It had been a long day. Loading the trucks and sorting all the household goods had left her sore and achy, but also filled with a sense of accomplishment. She'd considered helping with the moving-in process, but decided she'd better save some of her strength for her own project. If it weren't for Reid's help, she didn't think she'd be looking at opening the place in only a couple of weeks. Several guests had already booked, though she wasn't so concerned at this point with filling the rooms.

All the delays in construction had already caused her to miss her original deadline of mid-September to snag the visitors who came for the big Founder's Day festival. Her next goal was simply to open, and then focus on bookings for Dover's huge Christmas Glory Lights display, which attracted more and more visitors every year.

The sound of Reid's truck pulling into the drive brought a smile to her face. He must have stayed till the very end. She'd been constantly distracted by him all day. Watching him was more interesting than sorting baby clothes and labeling boxes. The only curious thing had happened late in the morning, when he had come inside with an angry scowl marring his angular features. He'd spoken to Seth, then they had both walked outside. She had no idea what was going on, but the look on Reid's face still bothered her. Was that what he looked like when he was undercover? Fierce? Dangerous? Threatening?

Her pulse quickened as he came through the gate and across the lawn to join her.

He was a handsome man. A kind man. A man she could fall in love with—if things were different.

His gait was stiffer than normal. Like her,

he'd probably overdone it today. "You must be worn-out."

He nodded, leaning against the support post of the glider. "There was talk of waiting to clean up until tomorrow, but we decided we'd rather get it all done now."

"Good plan. Have a seat."

Gingerly he stepped onto the wooden platform, causing the swing to shift, then settled into the seat across from her. The swing was small and their knees kept touching. She tried to ignore the rush of warmth surging along her nerves.

"It was a good day. Seeing the faces of those families as we brought the donations into their homes made all the hard work worthwhile."

"I would have liked to see that."

"Mr. Reid! You're back." Lily raced across the lawn. "You didn't eat supper with us. How come?" She climbed into the glider and then onto his lap—something she'd never done before. Tori's eyes grew moist. The sight was so sweet. Her daughter truly loved this man.

"I was helping the people whose homes were flooded."

"That's what Mommy was doing, huh, Mommy?"

Tori's breath stuck in her throat. She bit her lip, fighting back tears. It was the first time Lily had called her Mommy. Her chest swelled with a warmth and love so intense it hurt, but part of her wondered if the child was already forgetting her real mother. It took two attempts before she could find her voice. "Yes." She stole a glance at Reid. His eyes were warm with understanding. He knew how special this moment was.

"Your mommy was a big help today."

"I want to help."

Tori tried to find her voice, but it was still squeezed tight with emotion. Reid came to her rescue.

"Okay. Next time we have a big project, we'll let you know."

"Good." Buster placed his paws on the glider platform and looked expectantly at Lily.

"I think Buster wants to play." Lily scooted off Reid's lap and charged out into the grass, giggling as the dog chased her.

Tori drew a shaky breath, burying her face in her hands. How could one word hold such powerful, life-altering emotion? She didn't think it possible that her love for Lily could be any greater, but being called Mommy took her heart to a new place. Deeper, higher, richer than she'd ever imagined.

The glider shifted as Reid moved over to her side of the swing. "Are you okay?"

She nodded, uncertain whether to smile or cry again. "She called me Mommy."

"Well, aren't you?"

"Yes, but I never thought, I mean, I don't want her to forget..." She swallowed, wiping fresh tears from her eyes.

"Don't overthink this, Tori. She loves you. It's only natural she'd call you Mommy eventually." He slipped an arm around her shoulders, and she rested her head against him.

"I didn't expect it to feel so overwhelming. I'm humbled and elated and scared and so happy."

"This is a big turning point in your life. I'm glad I got to share it with you."

The look in his brown eyes suggested he'd like to share more with her. She wanted that, too. But how could they when they were on opposite sides? "I really need to get Lily to bed." She tore her gaze from his and started to climb out of the swing. It shook and she staggered.

"Wait. Let me go first and I'll help you."

Before she could protest, he eased out onto the grass and extended his hand, flashing his heart-stopping smile again. She took his hand, his fingers closing around hers gently, and stepped forward. Her toe caught on the slats and she lurched forward. Strong arms grabbed her around the waist instantly, and she was lifted into them briefly before being set on the ground. He didn't release her, instead holding her close and staring into her eyes.

Like before, when he'd rescued her from the sunroom, she experienced an odd cord of connection. Only this time she understood what it was. He was going to kiss her, and she didn't want to stop him. She'd wondered about this moment for too long. But she couldn't let it happen.

"Thanks." She stepped away from him. The closeness warmed her through and through, and she needed space to catch her breath and dispel the fog of attraction that always clouded her mind when he was near.

"I'd better get Lily to bed. It's been a busy day for her, too."

He walked with her across the lawn, and she wished she could have him at her side always. Her cell phone rang and she slipped it from her pocket, inhaling sharply when she saw the name on the screen. She glanced at Reid.

"What is it?"

"My attorney." She accepted the call as butterflies took flight in her stomach. She listened, her pulse racing as he spoke. "Thank you. Thank you so much." She ended the call and looked at Reid. His brown eyes reflected his concern. She placed her hands on his chest, needing something to steady the floating-on-air sensation swirling inside her mind. "It's done. The inspector signed off on the house, and he withdrew his demand for a ramp. The funds will be released in a few days." She couldn't stop smiling. Overwhelmed with joy, she threw her arms around Reid's neck and gave him a fierce hug.

"Congratulations."

She lifted her face to say thank-you, but the friendly embrace changed and became something more. Her fingers lightly touched his bottom lip, then grazed the day-old stubble on his angular jaw. She looked into his brown eyes, darkened now to a simmering black. A small voice warned her to stop, but she ignored it. She wanted to kiss him, and she had a feeling once she did nothing would ever be the same. She whispered his name and he captured her mouth, his lips warm and tender. His kiss was filled with promise. Being in his arms felt right and safe and secure.

He ended the kiss, and she was grateful for the strength of his arms again as he held her close. Her knees were shaky and weak.

Suddenly uneasy about the moment, she stepped back, glancing around for Lily. Apparently, she'd gone inside, and the only witness to their kiss was a curious Buster, who sat at the foot of the porch steps. "I'd better go in. Lily..." She lost her words. She smiled at Reid, then turned and hurried into the house, every nerve in her body tingling. She stopped in the kitchen and placed cool palms against her warm cheeks.

Had she made a mistake in kissing Reid? Maybe, but she couldn't deny she'd never felt this way with the others. None of her fiancés had sent tingles to her toes or caused her bones to melt. Maybe they'd only been placeholders until Reid could come into her life.

But Reid was the wrong man. Wasn't he?

Then why did she keep seeing him on the fringes of her dreams? Why did she automatically include him in her plans for the future? Like a fast-growing wisteria vine, Reid had wound his way into everything at Camellia Hall. And she feared he'd done the same with her heart.

So what was she going to do about it?

Reid awoke with a start, shivering as the tendrils of his dream slowly untangled from his subconscious mind. Buster jumped up on the bed and burrowed under Reid's arm. "Hey, buddy." He scratched behind the mutt's ears, welcoming the company. Did the dog sense his turmoil?

Everything had changed today, and he was struggling to make sense of it. Which probably explained the nightmare that had awakened him at two in the morning. He'd been back undercover, blending in with the dark figures of that world. A fight broke out and he was pulled into the fray. A gun went off. He clutched his stomach, and the smirking face of Archer loomed over him as he started to fall.

The dream was in stark contrast to the one that had lulled him to sleep. That one had wrapped around him in softness and promise as he held Tori in his arms and kissed her, finding a sense of belonging he hadn't known since he was a child.

She'd lifted her arms and he'd bent down to give her a hug, but the moment her arms were around his neck everything changed. All he could see was the sweet curve of her jaw, the tempting lips and the cobalt eyes that held a smoky promise. She met him halfway, her fingers sliding up his neck to touch his hair. He could hold her in his embrace for the rest of his life.

Buster shifted and rested his head on Reid's chest, as if offering even more comfort.

But the shadows of his nightmare lingered,

refusing to relinquish their hold. He'd never anticipated his old life bleeding into this new one. There were dozens of criminals who would like to get revenge on him for shutting down their operations and sending them to jail. What if another one came to town? He'd always be looking over his shoulder, constantly worrying about Tori's and Lily's safety.

Kissing Tori had shown him the future he wanted, and her response had given him a sliver of hope that she might want it, too. But how could he in good conscience ask her to share a life that held the threat of danger every moment? Logically he knew he was exaggerating the situation. The bad-guy-out-for-revenge scenario was common in the movies and TV shows but rarely happened in real life.

But he'd have to tell her. If he didn't, he'd be guilty of withholding important information the same way he had when he'd first come to Camellia Hall. He was still trying to make up for that mistake. He couldn't add another.

"What are we going to do, Buster?" The dog whined.

He'd been instructed to be in Dallas on Tuesday, and he was already dreading it. Going back into that life would be like stepping into a foreign country. He'd cut those ties, shut the door and never looked back. But he had a job to finish. One last obligation.

On the other hand, given his confused emotions regarding Tori, time away from Dover would help him see things more clearly.

Tori set her cup of salted caramel mocha and the plate of maple pecan bars on the table at the Square Cup coffee shop. She and Shelley were stealing a few hours together sans daughters who were at a movie with Shelley's mother. They'd chosen a quiet table outside, on the edge of the patio, to enjoy the warm fall weather and the lazy pace of a quiet Sunday afternoon.

"I can't believe we both had time to get away." Shelley took a seat and exhaled a breath. "I'm in desperate need of some girl time."

"Me, too. I need to step back and sort things out. It's hard to do when Lily wants me watching her all the time."

"She'll get over that before long."

"I know. She's actually much better since Reid has been here, especially since he brought Buster home." Thinking about the dog pulled her back to the swing last evening and Reid's kiss. She'd relived the moment a dozen times during the night. She shouldn't have let it happen, but her internal scolding was pointless. She could no more have stopped him than she could stop breathing. Her insides warmed as she remembered the feel of his arms around her, his lips tender and firm on hers. She'd wondered about his kiss from the moment he'd plucked her off the plank and held her close.

"Hey." Shelley leaned forward, waving her hand in front of Tori's face. "Where did you go?"

Maybe she needed another perspective on things instead of running around her mind in circles. "I was thinking about something that happened yesterday."

Shelley peered closer. "Oh? Like what?"

She toyed with her coffee mug. "I kissed Reid. Well, he kissed me, but I guess I kissed him back."

A happy smile appeared on her friend's face. "It's about time."

"What are you talking about?"

"Oh, please. The attraction between you two is like watching bolts of lightning light up the sky. The only ones unaware of it are you and Reid. So, what was it like?"

She'd had no idea her feelings were so obvious. No sense in denying it now, though. "Nice."

Shelley shook her head. "What? A man like

that, and you say he kisses nice? Nope. He'd be a one-and-done, never-anything-like-it-in-my-life kind of kisser."

Tori blushed. It was true, but she wasn't ready to admit it, even to herself. It would remain her shameful secret. "I shouldn't have let it happen."

"Why not? You like him, don't you?"

"Yes, but that's the problem. I've always been too easily attracted to handsome, compelling men. Look how things went with Steve."

Shelley waved her hand. "Oh, please. That first fiancé of yours was nothing more than mutual attraction. He charmed you like he did all the other women he met."

"Which didn't stop, even after he gave me a ring."

"Right, and what about David? He was so obsessive, so controlling that you were afraid to speak your mind. I was so relieved when you ended that relationship."

"Which brings us to Will. The fraud, the liar, the con artist and manipulator."

"I know. He had us all fooled." Shelley took a bite of her pastry. "Wait. Are you thinking Reid is like Will? No way. Never."

"You don't even know him."

"I know enough. I've seen how helpful he is

around the place and the town. I've seen him with Lily and I've seen how he looks at you. He's as real and honest as it gets."

"Need I remind you he lied to me the moment he arrived here? And he's the brother of the man who abandoned my friend."

"I remember, but he hasn't lied since then, has he? Tori, you have to stop trying to put Reid into the same slot as his brother. It's not fair."

Life wasn't fair. She started to point that out to her friend, but Shelley reached out and grabbed her wrist.

"I think it's time for a mini-intervention. You need to stop pushing Reid away. He's not his brother, and you have to stop trying to be Judy. Lily needs you to be her mom, and you can't do that if you're not being true to yourself. Judy isn't here. You are. Lily has called you Mommy. Now let that reassure you that you're doing a good job, and relax and enjoy your child. Trust me when I tell you—kids grow up so fast. Emily's older brother is going to be nine. My little boy is gone. Don't waste any more time on what-ifs and trying to live up to the expectations of someone else's ideals."

It was good advice, and she should take it. Truth be told, she had already started letting go of the way Judy had done things in favor of her own way. So far she'd seen no ill effects from the changes. In fact, Lily was responding well to a more structured way of doing things.

"Lily asked again why she didn't have a daddy."

"What did you tell her?"

"I distracted her with something else."

"Tori, you're just making things harder. You might be able to distract her at age five, but what about when she's fifteen?"

Tori shook her head, then took a sip of her coffee. She didn't want to think that far ahead.

"Were you and Judy friends for a long time?"

"Since eighth grade. We went to college together, but she transferred after her freshman year so we lost touch for a while. She sent me a Christmas card, and we started the friendship up again."

"What was she like then?"

"Nice, fun to be with. She had a troubled home life. Her dad ran out on her when she was ten. She would get so angry when she spoke of him."

"Like she did when she talked about Lily's father?"

"Yes." Why had she not made the connection sooner? Had Judy mentally combined her hurt and anger at her father with Eddie's desertion? It would account for her intense emotions whenever he was mentioned. Add to that her cancer treatments and knowing she was losing the battle. She probably wasn't thinking rationally at all. But did that absolve Tori from keeping her end of the bargain?

Every day her situation with Reid and Eddie grew more complicated and confusing.

The aroma of fresh coffee drew Reid to the kitchen. Tori's coffee was the highlight of his morning—that and eating breakfast with his adorable little niece. Lily was perched on one of the kitchen stools eating cereal. He smiled and gently stroked her silky hair. "That looks good." Lily usually expounded on the food she was eating, telling him how Tori had made it and how yummy it was. Today she didn't respond at all. Concerned, he took a seat beside her. "What's up, Lily? Something on your mind?"

She nodded, her bottom lip puckered out. "I want my mommy to come back."

Reid's chest tightened. He was not the right person to have this discussion. He was way out of his depth. "I know, but she can't, Lily. You know that."

"I want her back. I miss her."

"You have Tori now. She loves you very much."

"She's my new mommy. I miss my old one. I don't want her to be in heaven."

He knew only too well how the little girl felt. "My mommy is in heaven, too. And I miss her every day."

"Do you want her back?"

"Sometimes. But I know she's happy with Jesus, and I want her to be happy."

Lily started to cry, and Reid instinctively lifted her onto his lap. She shifted and wrapped her arms around his neck as she cried. "It's okay to miss her, Lily. Why don't you tell me about your mommy and I'll tell you about mine?"

The little head nodded. Reid pulled a napkin from the holder and wiped her tears.

"Lily, it's time to get ready for school."

Reid glanced up and met Tori's concerned gaze. He dabbed at Lily's tears and gave her a little squeeze. "We'll talk about our moms after school. Okay?"

Lily nodded, then reached her arms out for her mother. Tori gathered her close. "I love you, Lily."

"I love you, too, Mommy."

Tori caught his eye and mouthed, *Thank you.*

He had the oddest sense of accomplishment. He'd helped Lily and pleased Tori. Maybe he could handle this family-man thing after all.

After Lily left the room Tori faced him, her blue eyes filled with worry. "What happened?"

"No idea. She was eating her breakfast, and suddenly she stopped and wanted Judy."

Tori nodded. "I never know what will trigger her sadness. For a while it was rain. She'd cry and huddle in my lap until it stopped. It was raining thc day Judy died, so I guess in her mind there was some kind of connection. Poor little thing can't understand death. I wonder if I should have stayed in California, where things were familiar to her. I thought it was best to start over, and I needed the help of my family. But now I'm wondering."

Reid sat down. "You're being too hard on yourself. You're doing a great job. You just need to trust your judgment."

"That's what scares me. My judgment hasn't been very good over the years." She stared at the countertop, idly rubbing a spot on the surface. "I didn't want to become Lily's guardian. I tried to tell Judy it was a bad idea, but she insisted. How could I refuse her dying request?"

He hadn't expected that. "Why didn't you want to be her guardian?"

"Because I didn't want to let Judy down, or Lily. You know my track record, three failed relationships and a string of unrelated careers."

Was she saying she wanted out of her guardianship? "Do you still feel that way?"

"No. I love Lily. But at the time, the responsibility of raising her was terrifying, and I didn't feel I could handle it."

He'd heard this song before. The tune was familiar. "I imagine my brother felt much the same way when Judy told him she was pregnant. The responsibility of parenthood and being a husband must have been overwhelming to a man who'd been aimless most of his adult life."

The stunned look in Tori's eyes revealed his remark had hit home. He had no desire to hurt her when she was feeling vulnerable, but he had little time left to give Eddie what he wanted most. The glare she sent in his direction burned all the way to his soles. He watched her walk away, stiff-backed and hands fisted at her side.

He was out of ideas on how to make her see. The only thing left was heartfelt prayer.

Reid's truck was missing from the driveway when Tori returned from taking Lily to school. She'd lost her irritation toward Reid, and even had to admit his comment had been painfully true. She had wanted to run from responsibility the same way his brother had. The difference was, she'd stepped up despite her fears. Eddie had turned tail and run. Sadly, though, she now had insight into Lily's father, which rounded off another of his hard edges.

Tori welcomed the silence of the old home. She needed time to think. About Reid, about herself and about how to resolve their impasse. A glance at the repair list suggested Reid had probably gone to the hardware store. It had become an ongoing joke. He made at least three trips daily to the store and was on a first-name basis with the owner and the employees.

An unfamiliar ringtone rose into the air. Reid's phone was on the counter. It wasn't like him to forget it. She debated whether to answer it or let it go to voice mail. But what if the call was important? She glanced at the name on the screen—and winced. Eddie. Reid's brother. Maybe she should answer in case something was wrong. Scooping up the phone, she hit the accept button. "Hello."

Silence hung heavily on the other end. She waited a moment longer.

"Is this Miss Montgomery?" The voice was soft and a bit shaky.

"Yes."

"This is Eddie, Reid's brother."

"I know who you are."

"Yes, of course. I'm glad to have a chance to talk to you."

Here it comes. The plea for her to change her mind.

"I wanted to tell you how much I appreciate you taking care of my little girl. It's a wonderful thing you've done, becoming her guardian. Reid has told me how devoted you are to her. It gives me tremendous peace knowing she'll be raised by someone who loves her as much as her mother did."

Not what she'd expected. She sank onto the kitchen stool. "Thank you. She's a very sweet child."

"I'm sure. Her mother was a sweet woman." Muffled coughing broke his speech. "I want to thank you for allowing Reid to take pictures of my girl. She's a real beauty."

Tori didn't want to hear this. She steeled herself to remain detached. "Can I take a message? Reid ran to the hardware store. He should be back any moment."

"No. I just wanted to hear his voice. I get

lonely sometimes. He's always a great comfort. Just tell him I called."

"I will."

"Miss Montgomery, I want you to know I pray for you and for Lily every day."

"Thank you. That's very kind."

"God bless."

Tori stared at the phone after the call ended. Eddie Blackthorn wasn't the heartless monster she'd envisioned. He had sounded sincere, kind and genuine. She wanted to doubt his humble words but couldn't. The man was dying. She heard it in the breathless tone of his voice.

A swell of compassion touched her heart. For the first time, she wondered if there was an expiration date on loyalty. What if Eddie died and then she regretted not letting them meet?

No. She had to honor Judy's request. She had good reasons. Eddie might seem nice now, but that didn't excuse what he'd done in the past. So why didn't she feel the sense of righteousness she normally experienced?

Reid entered the kitchen a short while later with a bag of items he needed to finish the bathroom in the blue room. "There it is. I can't believe I left my phone here."

Tori crossed her arms over her chest. "Your brother called."

Reid's expression sobered. "Is he okay?"

"Yes. He wanted to talk to you, that's all."

"Wait. You talked to him?"

"I thought it might be serious so I answered."

"What did he say?"

She measured her words. "He thanked me for taking care of Lily. And he said he'd pray for us."

"He's deeply grateful for that. No matter what you may think of him, he only wants the best for Lily. He's not the same man he once was. His faith has changed him. All he's asking is…"

Tori held up her hand. "Don't." She couldn't look at him. She knew in the back of her mind he was right, but she wasn't ready to toss aside a promise made to a dying friend.

Reid slipped the phone into his pocket and picked up the bag. "I'll be upstairs if you need me."

Tori bit her lip. Why had she answered the phone? Lily's father had always been some distant boogeyman off in the distance, a menace to be avoided at all costs. That image was shattered now. It was easy to hate him and to stand her ground about keeping Lily away. But how could she do that now, knowing the man was showing her more forgiveness and compassion than she'd been willing to give him?

Yet, as Lily's guardian, she didn't have the right to override Judy's wishes. Did she?

Chapter Ten

Tori bit her lip and lifted her hair off her neck, taking a deep breath. Frustration had her clenching her jaw as she scrolled through her contact list for the third time. None of the people she counted on for babysitting were able to help. She should have had someone lined up sooner, but it had never been a problem before. Maybe she shouldn't have waited until an hour before the meeting to start looking.

Reid stopped at the counter when he saw the scowl on her face. "Everything okay? You look stressed."

She frowned and held her phone up. "You would think with three brothers and their wives in town, my mother, a neighbor and several close friends, someone could watch

Lily today so I can get to the crafters guild meeting this afternoon."

"Is the meeting important?"

"Yes. I wanted to lay out my idea for the gift shop and get their reaction. If there's no interest, then there's no point in making plans."

He hiked up one shoulder. "I'll watch her. I was going to work in the yard this afternoon. Lily will be outside playing anyway. What time do you have to go?"

She glanced at the clock. "I have to be there in forty-five minutes. I shouldn't be gone more than an hour and a half, tops."

"Perfect. Go. I got this."

What was wrong with her? She was actually considering leaving Lily with him. "I don't think so."

He crossed his arms over his chest. "Are you afraid I can't take care of her?"

"You don't have much experience with children." She scrolled through her contact list again.

"True, but Lily and I get along well. And I have first-aid experience in case it's needed."

"That's *not* reassuring."

He chuckled and waved her away. "Tori. Go. It'll be fine."

If the meeting wasn't so important she would have simply skipped it, but her business doomsday clock was ticking. "Fine. But promise you won't take your eyes off her."

All through the meeting, Tori tried to ignore the anxiety in her chest. Thankfully, the guild members were thrilled with her idea for a gift shop featuring their work on consignment. Her mood floated happily in the air as she made her way home. Things were finally looking up. The house was ready, the repair list was dwindling and she was starting to get inquiries on the website for reservations.

Tori parked beside Reid's truck and entered the gate to the backyard. Buster didn't come to greet her, which meant they must be inside. "I'm home." She dropped her purse and the satchel of folders onto the kitchen table, aware of an odd silence in the house. No TV sounds, no giggles, no sense of life at all. A chill chased down her spine. "Lily! Reid?"

A quick search through the rooms upstairs and downstairs revealed an empty house. Every nerve in her body burned. He'd taken her. All his reassurances had been lies. She fought the urge to curl up in a ball and cry. She didn't want to believe Reid would take her daughter. She'd come to care for him, more than she'd like, but here she was repeating her old pattern of picking the wrong man.

She had to find Lily. That was all that mattered. She dashed outside, looking at the glider swing and the apartment in case they were there. Empty.

Her throat filled with a scream. Her chest constricted. "Lily!" *Oh, God, show me where she is. Help me find her.* She pulled out her phone and brought up Seth's number, her fingers shaking so badly she hit the wrong name twice.

A familiar giggle penetrated the darkness. Hope rose in her. "Lily?"

"Hi, Mommy."

She spun around to see her daughter waving happily as she walked up the drive with Reid, who had Buster on his leash.

Relief threatened to buckle her knees. Pushing through the gate, she ran to Lily, wrapping her in her arms. Tears streamed down her cheeks.

"Mommy, you're squeezing me too tight."

"Tori? What's going on?"

She stood, keeping a hand on Lily's shoulder, needing the contact to keep her calm. When her gaze met Reid's, she realized what she'd done. His dark eyes reflected his confusion. "I came home and no one was here. I thought you'd..." She bit her tongue to stop the accusatory words.

"We took Buster for a walk." Reid's eyes

darkened. "You thought I'd taken her to see Eddie without asking you."

"I'm sorry, I just—"

"You just don't trust me. You never will." He set his hands on his hips, his mouth set in a hard line. "I know how much you love Lily. I would never put you in the position of fearing for her safety. Whether you believe it or not, I love her, too. I want what's best for her. So does my brother."

"I know."

Lily took her mother's hand. "Buster made a new friend on our walk."

She squeezed the little hand and smiled. "He did?"

"Uh-huh. Her name is Willow, and she's little and white and really fuzzy."

"Her?"

"Apparently Buster has a way with the ladies."

Reid's comment eased some of the tension, but she couldn't ignore the undercurrent of hurt in his tone. "I'll bet Buster is thirsty after his walk. Why don't you give him some fresh water in his bowl?"

Lily raced off, dog in tow, leaving her alone with Reid. "I apologize. I overreacted when I didn't find you here." She swallowed at the stern expression on his face. This was the old

Reid, the hard, closed-off man who'd arrived at her home that first day.

His jaw worked side to side before he spoke. "I don't know what else I can do to convince you I'm not going to go against your wishes. That doesn't mean I won't stop praying you'll change your mind."

"I can't. It would be a betrayal of my friend's dying wish."

"And I'm trying to grant my brother's dying wish. So how do we get beyond this impasse?"

"I wish I knew. I don't want to be the bad guy in this."

"Neither do I." He took a deep breath. "You don't have to worry about me taking Lily away from you. I'd be a lousy father."

"Don't say that. You're great with Lily, and she thinks the world of you."

"The truth is, I've spent the last decade living among the worst of society. I'm not sure I know how to live with honest, decent people anymore."

"Is that why you lied to me in the beginning?"

He rubbed his forehead. "When you're undercover you have to think on your feet, create believable reasons for your actions or words, anything to protect your cover. I didn't know you or how you were treating my niece.

I thought I could get a better read on you if you didn't know who I was. It was a bad decision and I regret it."

Reid looked into her eyes. "You're doing a great job with Lily. You're an amazing mother. Don't ever doubt that. I wouldn't deprive Lily of that for anything. Not even a visit to Eddie."

"I know. I'm sorry I jumped to conclusions, but my last relationship taught me a few hard lessons about trusting men."

"What happened?"

"He turned out to be a phony all the way around. He wasn't a high-powered executive, he didn't want a family, he didn't really love me and he wasn't a Christian. Oh, he talked the talk, but it was all a lie. Everything about him was a lie." She wrapped her arms around her waist. Might as well share the worst part. "Including being single."

"Tori, I'm so sorry. I haven't been lying to you. I didn't tell you who I was, but I've never lied."

She nodded. "I know."

Reid smiled at her, then started toward the house. "I have to leave for Dallas tomorrow. I don't know how long I'll be gone."

"We're supposed to open in less than two days."

"I know. And I'll get back as soon as I can.

There are only a few repairs left, and none of them are major."

When had she started counting on Reid to be at her side for the opening? His time with her was almost up. Her funds were on the way, and there were no more obstacles to her moving forward with her dream. And it was time to cut ties with her handyman. She lifted her chin and gathered her inner determination. "Thank you for your help. I couldn't have done it without you."

For all their sakes, she needed to keep a measure of distance. No matter how she might feel. "We'll see you when you get back. We'll need to settle up your pay then. I have a feeling I'm going to owe you a lot of money."

His wounded expression ripped through her. "Sure. Well, I need to pack. I leave early in the morning."

"Okay."

She watched him walk away, her heartstrings twisting painfully with every step he took.

It was best this way, keeping it professional. So why did she have tears in her eyes and a feeling she was making a huge mistake?

On the porch she glanced back at the apartment. Did Reid really think he'd be a bad father? His admission had given her a glimpse into his vulnerable side. She could understand how living in a criminal environment could cause him to lose sight of the goodness within him. She wished she could make him see how wonderful he was, how much he'd changed since coming to Camellia Hall.

Day by day she'd seen his hard edges soften, his reserved nature opening up. She attributed most of the change to her daughter. Lily had a way of turning the hardest hearts to mush.

She had to find a way to make up for assuming the worst about Reid. Had she taken a moment to think, she might have noticed the dog's leash missing from the peg near the back door. And realized that Reid would never take Lily or do anything to hurt her. But she'd jumped to conclusions, hurting Reid in the process and driving a wedge between them, which had only widened their impasse.

Maybe with Reid gone for a few days she could come up with a way to smooth over the mess she'd made. The obvious solution, however, was one she wasn't ready to embrace. Allowing Lily to meet her father would mend the rift between her and Reid, but it would leave her with a burden of guilt she wasn't ready to carry.

There had to be some other way.

* * *

Reid shoved his small satchel into the overhead and took his seat beside the window. He hoped his seatmate wasn't the chatty type because he had a lot to think through. Tori's reaction to coming home to an empty house spoke volumes about her real feelings. He'd been hoping their relationship had reached a new level of trust and she would understand he wasn't going to hurt her or Lily.

Now it was clear she would always see him as the enemy, someone who would walk away and break her heart. Her revelation about her last fiancé had given him a better understanding of her strong resistance to trusting him. He couldn't imagine a man taking advantage of Tori's sweet nature, though niceness only made her the perfect victim for a con artist. The guy had wounded her deeply and left her with a fear of trusting that she might never overcome.

It made winning her heart twice as hard for him. He already had so many strikes against him. He didn't blame Eddie, but without his brother's past behavior between them, there might have been a chance. But then, without Eddie he never would have met Tori in the first place. Or his little niece.

His gaze drifted to the window, and he

watched absently as the plane began to taxi. Maybe it was time to think about moving on. Soon the bed-and-breakfast would open. The funds would be deposited in the bank, and Tori could move forward and make a success of her business. He wasn't needed any longer.

His trip to Dallas was coming at a good time. The break would help him adjust his perspective. He needed space to think. Time away from emotional ties. There was also the appearance of Archer to consider. Seth was keeping a close eye on things while he was gone, but it had created a new worry. He loved Lily. And he was pretty sure his heart was already lost to her beautiful mother, and that meant he wanted to protect them at all costs. Even if it meant protecting them from himself and his past. If a future with Tori meant putting her at risk, in danger of becoming a target for the scores of criminals he'd put away, then he'd rather walk away and keep them safe.

His old life could never touch them. Ever.

It was probably for the best. Tori's world was family, love and togetherness. His had always been alone, in the underworld. Could he ever shed his dark past and learn to live a different way? His life had been all about the adrenaline rush, the danger, the triumphant moment when he took down the bad guy. Could family life offer anything like that? Would he miss the danger, the challenge?

But the thought of returning to his old life left a sour taste in his throat, forcing him to question whether he was fit for either world.

Tori opened the door to her bedroom closet looking for a box of jewelry she'd placed there, but it was the box on the floor in the corner that snagged her attention. Grief lowered her shoulders. The carton was filled with the few personal belongs Judy had possessed. Tori had intended to go through it and see if there were things she should preserve for Lily, but had never found the time.

After tugging the box out into the room, she sat on the bed and opened the flaps. Her grief still burned for her friend. Even after all these months, it was still strong. Judy had packed the box, so Tori was curious to see what she'd saved. A box of jewelry was the first item she lifted out. A quick check told her she'd sort through it and save the pieces for Lily. One of Lily's baby blankets, along with a few infant clothes, were folded together neatly. Beneath them were several children's books Tori remembered reading to Lily. A Bubble Wrapped figurine of a little girl holding a basket of flowers was next. At the bottom she found a large brown envelope. She lifted it out, moving to the armchair to sort through its contents.

Much of it was duplicates of insurance papers, Judy's will, the guardianship papers Tori had signed and a few other legal documents. The originals were all with Tori's attorney. She pulled out a paper-clipped stack of pictures Lily had drawn, scribbles from toddlerhood and a couple of handmade cards. The next item was a spiral notebook with Judy's name on it. She set it aside to look at later.

Only one thing remained. Tori slipped the paper from the envelope, her hands trembling as she read the large letters. *Certificate of Marriage.* The names below sent a jolt through her system. *Judith Marie Stevens. Edward Lee Blackthorn.*

Tori stared at the document, inhaling short, rapid breaths, making it hard to breathe. This couldn't be true. Judy had always said she and Lily's father were never married. Why would she lie about this? Had she hated him so much that she'd denied his existence?

Another thought shoved into her mind, and she closed her eyes against it. If Reid's brother was legally Lily's father, that meant he had rights. Parental rights he could exercise to force her to bring Lily to see him. Or—worse—to claim custody of the little girl.

This couldn't be happening. Why hadn't Judy told her the truth? What would Reid do when he found this out? He obviously knew. He'd mentioned it a couple of times, but she'd corrected him. Now she had proof in her hands, and she could see only disaster ahead.

She could pretend she'd never found it. Destroy the paper and move on. Her conscience flared. Then she wouldn't be any better than Reid, withholding important information. As much as she wanted to ignore the discovery, she couldn't live with herself if she did that. The smart thing to do would be to call her attorney. They'd already discussed her officially adopting Lily, but that had been down the road. Now she wanted to press forward. No one was going to take Lily away. Not even her biological father.

She pulled out her phone and placed the call to her attorney, wishing Judy had trusted her with the truth. It didn't make sense. Thinking back, there were many things Judy had done and said that didn't make sense, but Tori had accepted them as either a parent thing or a result of her ongoing cancer battle and the treatments. Now she was looking at them in a new light. What else had she missed?

Reassured after the conversation with her attorney, she went back to the box. Her good mood was shattered. She'd deal with these things later. She repacked the items, but held on to the notebook. It was a spiral stenographer's pad. She flipped over the cover and glanced at the contents. The first entry expressed Judy's shock at her diagnosis. Clearly she was scared, but hopeful. As she leafed through the pages, tears formed. Judy had tried to be so brave and talked about her dreams for Lily. But a third of the way in, the tone changed. Her words grew harsh, her anger more evident. Her focus shifted to Eddie and his abandonment. It became difficult to read her ferocious text. The more Tori read, the more confused she became. Judy's feelings about her husband bounced between missing him and feeling rage over his desertion.

What did it all mean? Her head spun with the possibilities. After replacing the box in the closet, she carried the notebook to her night table and slipped it into the drawer. She'd have to look at it again when she was thinking more clearly. Maybe she needed another perspective.

She picked up her phone and made arrangements for Shelley to come by after school. Lily and Emily could play and they could talk. By the time her friend showed up, Tori was ready to burst. She'd looked at the notebook again but it only confused her more.

Shelley curled up on the rattan sofa in the sunroom, her expression revealing her concern. "What's going on? I could hear the desperation in your voice through the text message."

"Sorry. I need another point of view on this."

"You said you found something?"

"Judy's marriage license."

Shelley frowned. "Which means what?"

"She lied to me. She always claimed she and Lily's father were never married. But they were, which means Lily's father has legal rights. He could take her away from me."

"What does your attorney say? Can't you adopt her?"

"Yes, but I have to get her father to relinquish his paternal rights. I doubt if Reid would let him do that."

"It sounds like you've done all you can for now. I'm sure your lawyer will get it all worked out."

"But there's more." She pulled out the steno pad. "I found this in her things, too. It's a journal of sorts, and she started it shortly after her diagnosis. She starts out writing about things she wanted to tell Lily, her fears and dreams."

"Sounds sweet. Are you going to give it to Lily someday?"

Tori shook her head. "It starts out sweet, but it ends up very different. Read this." She handed Shelley the pad, opened to an entry near the back. She watched her friend's expression go from curious to confused to horrified.

"This doesn't even make sense."

"I know. It makes me wonder about everything she told me. She lied about being married, and some of the things she railed about were untrue. It makes me wonder..."

"If there was really any reason to keep Lily from her dad?"

"It makes me question everything I thought I knew about Judy. I just don't know what I want to do about it. I'm thinking about not telling Reid any of this. At least until I have time to sort it all out."

Shelley shook her head. "Bad idea. If you're asking me for advice, then I say tell him everything. Neither of you can make good decisions based on lies and distortion."

"But I feel so disloyal."

"Tori. Believe it or not, loyalty can have limits. Judy counted on your loyalty to keep her anger going. But she lied about that. So you're free from honoring her requests. Are you going to be loyal to a woman who's dead, or to the child who is alive and here with you?"

Tori mulled this over. She felt as though she were caught in a trap—being a faithful friend versus being a good parent to Lily.

Pulling up into the drive of Camellia Hall had never felt more like coming home. But Reid's time here was almost up. He'd decided to make the most of the few days left and take one last stab at convincing Tori to let Eddie see Lily. He would be breaking their deal, but at this point he had nothing to lose. He also wanted to secure a promise from Tori that he could come and see his niece as often as possible.

He put his chances on the slim side, but he had to try. Time was short.

Buster greeted him as he entered the back gate through the picket fence, and he gave him a long scratch on his neck. "I missed you, too, fella." His spirits lifted like a hot-air balloon as he took the steps to the porch and reached for the doorknob. He'd missed Tori and Lily, too. Far too much. Leaving them would be harder than he'd ever imagined.

He tapped on the back door before entering. Tori was sitting at the small desk in the sunroom. She glanced up at him and smiled, turning his heart to warm syrup in his chest. Was she glad to see him? Or was she merely happy to have her hired help back? He shoved the thought aside as he sat on the rattan chair.

"Welcome back."

"Good to be back."

"Everything go well in court?"

"It did. The guy will be locked away for many years. How did things go here? Has my repair list grown out of control?"

"No. As a matter of fact, not one thing has broken, clogged up or worn out since you left."

Reid wished it had. He'd welcome an excuse to stay on a while longer. "Then I guess I'm almost done here." Her eyes darkened and she looked away, toying with the stapler on the desk.

A nagging twinge started in his chest. He knew that feeling. It always meant trouble. "And how's my Lily? It's only been a few days, but it's like I haven't seen her in months. The little princess wraps around your heart and won't let go."

Tori squirmed in the chair, keeping her eyes averted. Now he knew something was wrong. "Yes, she does. I'm afraid she's going to be a heartbreaker when she grows up."

"Too late. She already is." He leaned forward, resting his forearms on his knees. "You want to tell me what's going on? What happened while I was gone?"

She looked at him, her blue eyes filled with an odd mixture of sadness and guilt. Whatever she had to say wouldn't be good.

"I was going through some of Judy's things, and I found the marriage certificate."

He studied her a moment, uncertain of what she was trying to say. "Okay. Eddie always claimed they were but his memory isn't the best."

"But Judy always denied it. She swore up and down they were never married. She lied about it." She rested a hand against her cheek. "This changes everything."

"How?"

"Your brother now has legal claim on my daughter. His daughter. I have to tell you, I've already started the process of adoption for Lily, but since this has come to light it complicates things."

Reid nodded. "I guess it does. Eddie always said they were married, but he has a lot of blank spots in his memory so I figured he didn't really know. What does your attorney say?"

She took a deep breath before answering. "Eddie has to relinquish his parental rights before I can legally adopt Lily."

Reid was beginning to see where this was leading. He stood, his irritation mounting. "So you want to know if he'll do that and give you a clear path?"

"Wouldn't it be best for Lily?"

"Probably. But what about what's best for Eddie?"

"I don't know. Lily is my only concern."

"Yes. You've made that very clear. Maybe this would be a good time to discuss a compromise."

Tori bit her lip. "You mean visiting your brother."

"It seems like a fair trade. One visit in exchange for signing away his rights to his only child."

"You make it sound so cold and heartless. Like I'm buying her."

He hadn't meant to, but stepping back into his old world had reignited this attitude. "Well, those are the kind of situations I'm used to."

"Don't you want what's best for your niece?"

"I want what's best for all of us." He moved to the door. "I need to discuss this with Eddie."

"Will you ask him to do the right thing by Lily?"

"I'll ask. But you might not like the answer. Maybe it's time *you* did the right thing, Tori."

"I'll think about it."

"The time for thinking is over." He stomped out and climbed into his truck. This was not the homecoming he'd longed for, but it's what he should have expected. Tori was determined to keep her promise to her friend no matter what. This new information might give him leverage to force Tori to let Eddie see his child. He didn't like doing it this way, but he had no choice.

Reid watched the play of emotions across his brother's face later that day.

"I told you we were married. But my memory is spotty, so I thought maybe I'd only wished we were. Good to know I was right."

"You realize this changes things. You can petition the court to force Tori to bring Lily to see you."

"I can?"

"You're her legal parent. You have rights."

"Yes. I do. Reid, I want the Montgomery woman to bring my little girl here right away. If she refuses, I'll start some sort of legal process to make her."

"Is that really what you want to do?"

"No. But I want you to tell her so. Maybe it'll shake her out of her rut and get her to see how serious things are."

"Eddie, Tori has started adoption proceedings. But she can't legally adopt Lily unless you sign away your parental rights."

"No. I can't do that. Lily would think I didn't care about her at all. She'd hate me. She might even wonder what was wrong with her that I wrote her off. I know I've made a mess of things, but she should know I really loved her."

"What do you want to do?"

Eddie sank back into his pillow. "Maybe we should wait until I'm gone, then she can go ahead with her adoption. It won't matter."

A surge of denial flooded his throat. "Don't talk like that. I'll do whatever you want."

"I want to see my little girl. Time is running out. I can sense it. See what our options are. Maybe there's something else we can do. Maybe we can let her think we're taking action, only we're not."

Great. He was back to lying and manipulating Tori for his own ends. Every step he took added another row of bricks to the wall he was building between him and Tori. "All right. I'll look into it."

Reid stayed until his brother fell asleep, then went outside and placed a call to his attorney. He didn't want to take legal action against Tori. If he did, it would widen the divide between them and damage their relationship irrevocably. Eddie might get to see Lily, but Tori would never speak to him again.

Why did doing the right thing for Eddie have to be the worst thing for a woman he cared for so much?

Chapter Eleven

Tori looked out the window to the apartment. Reid was sitting on the small patio, staring at his phone and tossing a stick for Buster. He'd been back in Dover since early last night, but he hadn't said a word to her. Instead, he'd gone to the apartment and closed the door. Lily asked for him, but he didn't even come to see her.

Moving away, she sighed and paced the sunroom. The cozy space usually soothed her anxious thoughts and helped her see things more clearly. But this situation was far too complicated. She had no idea what Eddie had said about signing away his rights to Lily. The mere thought of someone doing that made her angry. How could any parent cut the ties and go on with their life as if the child had never existed? But if he didn't, then even after he passed, Reid would have more rights to custody of Lily than she would.

Maybe she should have agreed to the visit from the start, and then none of this would have happened. Eddie would be happy and Reid would have kept his promise. But her promise would have been broken. How would she have lived with herself, knowing she'd betrayed her friend?

Why was there no simple solution that would please everyone? Why did both choices involve breaking someone's trust?

Later that afternoon, the mailman brought a new book for Lily. With a few minutes free, Tori and Lily sat on the front porch in the rockers to read it. With the freshly painted rockers and a porch swing at either end, the space beckoned visitors to stop and sit for a spell and enjoy the peaceful surroundings. Her guests would love it, and she had Reid to thank.

Lily settled in her lap. "Maybe Mr. Reid can read to me now."

Tori ignored the disappointment swirling inside. Reid was still keeping his distance. "He has some work to do. He can read it to you later."

Snuggled up in the rocker, Tori began the

tale of a little girl who lived in a teeny tiny house with lots of teeny tiny friends.

Heavy footsteps sounded on the porch floor as she finished the story. Reid stopped in front of them and leaned against the post. “Was that a good book?”

Lily nodded vigorously. “The little girl in the story was named Lily. Like me.”

“That’s pretty cool.” He spoke the words to his niece, but his gaze was riveted on her. “When you have some time, I’d like to talk to you.” At least he wasn’t avoiding them any longer.

Her heart clenched. Was he going to tell her Eddie was claiming his child? She had no idea what she would do if that happened. Logically, all she had to do was take Lily to see her dad and it would all be settled. Why was she having so much trouble deciding what to do? Was Shelley right? Was she choosing to honor the wish of a dead friend over what might be best for her daughter?

“Mr. Reid, can you read me the story again? Please?”

Tori had to smile at the softening of Reid’s features at the request. The big strong man was no match for the sweet pleas of a little princess.

“Sure, but first you need to go feed Buster. I noticed there was no water in his bowl.”

She pouted but complied. "Okay, but I'm going to go fast." She broke into a run across the porch and through the front door.

"I talked to Eddie."

Tori held her breath. "And?"

"He's looking into his legal options. You have to know he'll do whatever it takes to see his child. He doesn't have time to wait for a decision." He touched her hand. "I'm sorry. I'm just trying to do what he wants."

"I know. I'd hoped to avoid a legal battle."

"You have the solution. It's in your power."

"I know but…"

"I'm back." Lily grabbed Reid's hand and tugged him toward a rocker. He eased in it and reached for the book. Then he froze, his expression hard and fierce. "Tori. Take Lily inside. Call Seth and tell him to get over here now. Stay inside and don't come out until I tell you."

"Why? What's wrong?"

He was staring across the street. She looked in that direction, but all she saw was one of the neighbors standing by the lamppost.

"Just do as I say. Please."

"Reid, you're scaring me."

"Tori. Go. Now."

Her body chilled at the harsh tone of his voice. She'd never seen him like this before.

Quickly she took Lily's hand and hurried inside. "Lily, go to our rooms and you can play with my jewelry for a while."

"But Mr. Reid was going to read to me."

"I know, and he will, but right now I have to make a call. I'll be right there." She tapped her phone and called her brother, giving him Reid's message.

Seth uttered a growl. "Must be Archer."

"Who's Archer?"

"Never mind. Stay inside. I'm on my way." He hung up, making her even more anxious.

Unable to resist, she walked to the front window and looked out. Reid was striding across the street, straight for the man. The guy spun and ran off, and Reid broke into a run, propelling himself through the air and tackling the man to the ground. The man resisted, but he was no match for Reid's strength. Reid forced the man onto his stomach, yanking his arms behind his back as Seth's patrol car skidded to a halt at the curb. Seth got out and in one quick motion put handcuffs on the man. Together, Seth and Reid raised the man to his feet, and Seth put him in the back of the cruiser.

After a few words with Reid, her brother got in the patrol car and drove off.

Tori turned away, realizing her hands were

shaking. Seeing Reid in action, doing what he was trained to do, was disturbing. He looked nothing like the man she knew. She wasn't sure what to do with this new perspective. There were things about Reid she would never know.

Heart racing, she waited inside the door for Reid to return. The grim look on his face scared her more than anything else. "What happened? Who was that man? What's going on?"

He took her arms in his hands and gently pulled her close. "It's all right now. His name was Cal Archer, a drug dealer I took down a few years ago. He was supposed to be in jail, but got released on a technicality. He came looking for me."

"Why?" Stupid question. Reid was a former agent. He probably had lots of enemies. "How did Seth know about him?"

"It's not the first time I'd seen him. He was at the warehouse the day we were loading the trucks for the flood victims. I checked up on Archer and let Seth know. He's been keeping an eye on you whenever I'm away."

"I had no idea."

"That's the point. I didn't want you to know."

"Thank you. Even when you're not here, you're watching out for us."

"You and Lily are important to me."

"I'd better go check on her." He walked with her to the private quarters, following her into the living room, where Lily was busy with the sparkly jewelry. "Does this sort of thing happen a lot? Criminals coming back to take revenge?"

"No. Rarely, if ever. It's not like on TV."

He was trying to reassure her, but the idea had been planted and she couldn't shake it off. He pulled her around to face him, one hand resting against her cheek. "I would never put you or Lily in any danger."

"I know." She laid her hand on his. Reid was a noble man, a man who would sacrifice his own life for those he loved or was responsible for. Of that she had no doubt.

His touch chased away much of her fear. Between Reid and her brother, she'd never felt safer. Nothing bad could touch them.

But what about their safety? She'd never seriously considered the risks Reid and her brother took. Dover was a quiet town with a low crime rate. But Reid had worked in a world where his life was on the line every second. The thought pressed hard against her lungs. What would she do if something happened to Reid?

What she saw today with the apprehension

of Archer was a clear sign she should put her barriers back in place. Or maybe she was simply a coward and afraid to risk her heart.

Reid wiped the excess grout from the last floor tile and sat back on his heels. His final repair was done. His to-do list was complete. Camellia Hall was ready to welcome guests. Oh, he knew something else would need fixing tomorrow—it was the nature of a house as old as this—but he wouldn't be here to take care of it.

He was out of work.

The soft opening of the Camellia Hall Bed-and-Breakfast was next week. Tori had invited family and a few close friends to come and spend the night to test out the menu and the hospitality so she could work through any bugs in her system. The official opening wouldn't be for another week after that.

The tightness in his chest twisted another notch. He'd expected to feel excited about the opening. He'd worked hard to get everything done, and he had a vested interest in seeing this business up and running. Mostly he'd looked forward to seeing Tori's joy as her dream became reality.

Only that was not how he'd been feeling. Instead, he'd been growing more and more restless. He'd grown too comfortable in Dover with Tori and Lily. He'd allowed himself to think about a different life, a normal future. But since the apprehension of Archer, everything had changed.

The things in the little town and the house that had filled him with peace now felt like a vine slowly wrapping around his body, choking off his air and making it impossible for him to break free. The idea gave birth to a fear he'd never known before, and one he didn't fully understand.

First thing Saturday morning Reid drove down to Hammond to see Eddie. His thoughts were as jumbled and cloudy as ever. He had to decide about his future. Where would he go from here? If Eddie wasn't sick, he'd buy that cabin for them to live in.

A future with Tori and Lily became less likely every day. Deep down he knew Tori would always see him as Eddie's brother—a man who could suddenly walk away. He knew she cared for him, but she would never take down the barrier between them, which left him with only one option. Time to move on. But the thought of returning to undercover work filled him with dread. He'd never intended to go back. But he had no plan for moving forward.

For the time being, he would spend every spare moment with Eddie. The doctors had said hospice care was imminent.

His brother was asleep when he slipped into his room. Just as well. Reid had a lot of thinking to do. When the phone rang, he quickly silenced it before answering. When he hung up, his chest had tightened a few more turns.

Eddie stirred and looked at him. "Hey. I was thinking about you."

"That so?"

"I think you're burdened."

For a man confined to a hospital bed and with few visitors, he saw a great deal. "What makes you say that?"

"I recognize the signs. I've experienced every one of them, and I don't want you to make the same mistakes I did."

Reid pulled the chair up to the bedside. "So enlighten me." He enjoyed these fatherly conversations with his brother. In many ways, though Eddie's life was shortened, he'd gained more wisdom than Reid ever would.

"You've changed. A lot. Before going to Dover and finding Lily and Tori, your life was fueled by anger and justice. Now it's fueled by love for my little girl and her lovely guardian. Am I right?"

Reid rubbed his forehead. "Yes, but I'm

not cut out for family life. I couldn't give them what they need. She's a forever kind of woman, and I'm not a forever kind of guy." But it was too late. He knew the truth. He was lying to himself.

"Not true. I see the change in you, brother. You have all you need. You love them. You need them. Tori has changed you. You can't deny that."

"No. I won't. When I first arrived at Camellia Hall, I didn't think I'd ever feel anything again. Undercover work killed any normal emotions I might have had."

"But she changed all of that?"

Reid nodded. "I didn't have a prayer. She got under my skin and there was no getting her out. She's strong and determined and resilient and warm and caring, and she makes everyone feel special. She makes me think I can be more, that I could be a normal person in spite of my past." He smiled. "And Lily, well, she stole my heart from the first moment I saw her."

"Sounds like a horrible situation."

Reid bristled until he realized Eddie was teasing. "It's been an experience. But it's over now, and time for me to move on."

"Why?"

"Eddie, Tori will never change her mind

about bringing Lily to see you. I've tried everything, but I'm afraid she'll always see me as—"

"The brother of the man who hurt her friend."

"Yeah. But it was Archer showing up that made me see how impossible a normal life would be for me. My past will always be hanging over us. I'll always be a lightning rod for the men I put away. I won't expose Tori and Lily to that."

Eddie waved a finger. "Not true. You're fabricating excuses."

"No, I'm not." He ran a hand down the back of his neck. "I thought when I found you and Lily I would find peace, but it doesn't feel like I'd expected."

Eddie held up a shaky hand. "First off, you won't find true peace in a family. Not even one with Tori and Lily. That kind of peace only comes from the Lord. We've talked about this."

"I know."

"So what are you going to do?"

Reid braced himself. His brother wouldn't like what he was going to say. "I've been asked to return to the DEA. I'm going to accept. It's time I moved on."

"You're making a mistake. The same one

I made. Don't do it. You'll always regret it." Eddie reached for his hand. "Don't be afraid of the emotions you feel. That was my mistake. When Judy told me she was pregnant, I was terrified. I didn't know how to be a dad. I remembered what a wonderful man our father was, and I could never measure up to him. Signing on for a lifetime commitment to Judy and the baby was terrifying. So I ran. Don't run from Tori. Don't go back to your old life. You're not that man anymore. And don't be afraid to step into a new one. Have you talked to Tori about this?"

"No."

"Don't be surprised if she gets upset."

Reid shook his head. "I think she'll be relieved." The thought hurt more than he'd expected. He wanted to think she'd miss him when he was gone. And what about Lily? How could he ever fill the spot in his heart she had filled?

"Reid, I've changed my mind. I don't want to force Tori to bring Lily here. Tell her I won't take any legal action, but I'm not signing my little girl away as if she doesn't matter." He sighed. "It'll all be settled soon enough."

Monday morning dawned bright and sunny, reflecting Tori's good mood. Next week at this time she'd be welcoming a few friends and family into the house as her first guests for a dry run, to check for little glitches and iron out any missteps in hospitality before accepting real guests. And everything was ready. Thanks to Reid, the yard looked like a park, and the camellia bushes were budding as if in anticipation of the new life the old house would enjoy.

Even the repair list was complete. She hadn't added a single item in two days. Reid had gone to Hammond to be with Eddie. She understood his desire to spend as much time with his brother as possible, but a part of her missed him when he was gone. The house never felt as vibrant without him. Having his male energy in the house gave it a sense of permanence, of stability.

As if reading her mind, Reid's truck pulled into the drive. She couldn't stop the big smile that overtook her in anticipation of seeing him again. It was nice to have him home. Did he think of Camellia Hall as home? He'd grown more and more comfortable here. One of the most enjoyable times of her day was when the three of them gathered around the table to share the evening meal.

She glanced up as he came through the door, an exuberant Buster trotting beside him.

He smiled, his brown eyes seeking hers. “Hi.”

“Good morning.”

“How’s Eddie?” Despite her personal stance toward Reid’s brother, she fully sympathized with his emotional turmoil. She knew the agony of watching a loved one slowly slip away, and she wished she had some comforting words for him.

“Holding his own for now. He wanted me to tell you he’s changed his mind about taking legal action where Lily is concern, but neither will he agree to sign away his rights to Lily.”

“Oh. I see.” She was relieved Eddie wasn’t going to demand he see his daughter, and she wasn’t surprised he didn’t want to sign away his rights. But that left her in legal limbo.

“Do you? In a few weeks this will all be a moot point, won’t it?”

Like a stab to her heart, his words cut open the depth of her selfishness. Reid was losing the only family he had left, and she was adding to his burden.

“Forgive me. I’ve handled this whole thing badly. I wish Judy hadn’t put me in this position.”

Reid’s eyes softened. “I understand. So does Eddie. We’re all just trying to do what’s right for everyone.” He pulled a piece of paper from his back pocket, one she recognized as his to-do list. "I meant to leave this with you before I left. Anything new to add?"

She shook her head. "Nope. We've had a repair-free couple of days. Isn't that wonderful?"

His expression sobered. His dark eyes filled with regret. "Then I guess it's time for me to move on."

Her mind rejected the idea. "What do you mean? I thought you might stay on and maybe..."

Maybe what? *Love me and Lily, help me run the B and B?* That wasn't something they had discussed. It was all in her fanciful imagination.

"I'm going back to work, Tori. I have a new undercover assignment in Houston. I'll be leaving tomorrow so I can be briefed on the situation."

Reid. Gone. She hadn't expected the disappointment to be so sharp. But her fear for him pushed it aside. "No. You can't go back."

"It's done. The deal was I'd stay until the opening. The list is complete, so there's no reason for me to hang around."

"No, I mean you can't go back to that life. It's too dangerous."

"It's what I do."

"No. That's what you *used* to do. You're not that person anymore."

"What are you talking about?" Had Eddie been talking to her?

"You're calmer and more relaxed, and you aren't the hard-edged man who came to my house that first day. If you try to go back to undercover work, you could get killed."

He held up a hand for her to stop. "Okay, I know my skills might be a little rusty, but they'll come back."

"Why do you want to go back to that life? I thought you'd found something better here with—in Dover."

He rubbed his forehead. "I'll be back to visit as often as I can. I don't want to lose touch with Lily."

That was sweet, but her heart screamed, *What about me?* She realized in that moment that she cared more deeply for him than she ever had for anyone. But she'd waited too long to see it, and now he was walking out of her life and into a world that could get him killed.

The thought turned her blood to ice. "Please don't do this."

He came to her, cradling her face in his hands. "I'd like nothing better than to stay here with you and Lily, but we both know I'm not cut out for this kind of life. I don't know how to live a normal life or be a father. Besides, I could never live with myself if anything happened to you or Lily because of me."

"You mean Archer? You said that rarely happens."

"Rarely is still too big a risk."

He pulled her close and kissed her, and her heart sank. It was a kiss of goodbye. A kiss made to become a memory, not one filled with promise for a future.

"Reid?"

"I need to pack. I'll stay until Lily gets home so I can say goodbye. Oh, and if it's okay, I'd like to give Buster to her. I can't take a dog with me, and Buster would never forgive me if I took him away from her."

Tori's eyes blurred and she nodded.

"Tori. You don't need any help. You're going to be a great innkeeper, and you're already a wonderful mother."

Reid pivoted and walked out. Tori placed a hand over her mouth to keep from sobbing out loud. She'd finally achieved everything she'd worked for, but it held little satisfaction if Reid wasn't here to share it with her.

It was something she'd never anticipated. In the past she'd been the one to walk out on her fiancés. She never considered how it would feel if someone walked away from her.

And what about Lily? Would Reid's departure start her grieving process all over again?

Why hadn't she been more open, more practical, more compassionate? Shelley was right. Loyalty did have an expiration date.

Reid slid his duffel bag onto the back seat of his truck and shut the door at the same time Tori pulled in the driveway. Lily waved at him from the window and started tugging at her seat belt. His heart swelled with affection, knowing she was anxious to get to him. He wasn't looking forward to telling her he was leaving. He opened the car door and Lily reached for him, wrapping her little arms around his neck in a tight hug. He experienced a rush of love so profound that it stole his breath.

"I missed you so much. I'm glad you're home."

Home. If only. "I missed you, too, Lily. How about we go sit on the porch and talk for a minute, okay?" She nodded with a big smile, glancing down at Buster, who was sitting patiently at Reid's feet.

For fear of losing his resolve, Reid didn't make eye contact with Tori as he carried Lily to the porch. Leaving was the right thing to do for all of them.

Settled in one of the rockers, the little girl in the other, Reid searched for the words to begin. "Lily, the house is ready and I've fixed all the broken things."

"I know. Now the bee bees can come."

"That's right, and you'll have fun helping Mommy take care of them. But that means it's time for me to go."

Her dark eyes widened. "Why?"

"I have to go back to my real job."

"Where is it?"

"In a big city, far away." The sadness on her sweet little face tore at his heart.

"I won't see you anymore?"

"Not every day like you do now, but I'll be back to visit you."

Tears formed in the little eyes. "I don't want you to go. I told Emily I was going to ask you to be my daddy."

Oh, Lord, give me strength. "You were?"

"I told Emily I didn't have a daddy and she said everybody *had* to have one, so I was going to pick you 'cause I love you so much and you make me happy inside."

If he was being tested, he might just fail. How could he leave this precious little one behind? He glanced up and saw Tori standing discreetly at a distance, listening. Her eyes were moist, so she could probably hear them, as well.

"You make me happy, too, Lily." He lifted her from the rocker and placed her in his lap. "But I'm going to leave Buster here to keep you company. He'll be your dog from now on."

"Really?"

The dog placed his paws on Reid's knees, as if aware he was being discussed. "I know you'll take good care of him and give him lots of love."

"I'd rather love you." Her tears turned to sobs, and Reid looked at Tori for help. He had no idea how to comfort the little one.

She stepped forward and took Lily from his arms. "It's okay, Lily. Mr. Reid will come and visit us. He'll be one of our guests, and we can fix him a special breakfast. Won't that be fun?"

Lily didn't respond. She nestled her head in Tori's neck, looking forlorn.

Reid stood, his body feeling like it was made of lead, his heart cold as a stone. "I have to go." Tori nodded, but only made eye contact briefly.

After a quick pat on Buster's head, he spun

around and hurried off the porch and into his truck, then hurriedly cranked the engine. If he didn't pull away now, he never would, and that would be a mistake.

He maneuvered his truck through the streets of Dover, aware of the cord attached to Tori and Lily, a cord that stretched tighter with every mile he moved away from Camellia Hall. He was doing the right thing. He was.

A call showed up on his car's Bluetooth screen. Tori. "Hey, is Lily okay? Something happen?"

"No, Lily is okay. She's curled up with Buster in the sunroom. I wanted to ask you to please keep in touch with us. Maybe you could FaceTime Lily. But I also wanted you to let me know about Eddie. I'll be here to talk when—I mean if you need someone after..."

Could his heart take any more pain? "I will. I promise."

"Good. Thank you. And, Reid, I want you to know how important you've become to me as a friend."

His throat closed up. "Same here."

"Okay, then. Goodbye. Take care of yourself."

He ended the call, unable to bear the sound of her voice any longer. She sounded as emotionally distraught as he was. It took all his resolve not to turn the truck around and go back to the people he loved.

Chapter Twelve

Reid struggled to focus on the mission his superior, Leonard Novak, was outlining. The drive to Houston yesterday had been long and torturous. He'd questioned his decision with every rotation of the tires. His head told him it was best to step away from Tori's and Lily's lives. They had a large family to care for them and pick up any slack left by him. Trying to change his lifestyle, change who he was, would be too disruptive and only make things harder on the two people he loved most in the world.

But his heart had refused to be still, and the farther from Dover he drove the more he yearned to go back. The memory of Lily's tears when he'd said goodbye still left a sharp sting in his chest. The look of sadness and concern in Tori's eyes created doubts about his choice with every breath he took. But it was the right thing to do.

"Hey, Blackthorn. Are you listening?"

Reid slammed the door on his wayward thoughts. "Yes, sir."

"Good, because this job won't be easy." He leaned forward, tapping the folder on his desk with his finger. "We think the Russian mob has infiltrated the Benton gang in Lubbock. They're using a local fast-food restaurant as a cover."

Lubbock? That was even farther from Dover than he'd expected. How would he get back to check on Eddie?

"Something wrong?" Novak peered at him over the rim of his glasses.

"I wasn't expecting to be so far away."

"From what?"

Everything I care about. Suddenly the idea of going undercover, of living a lie, of wallowing in the dregs of humanity was abhorrent. His spirit craved the peace and sense of purpose he'd found in Dover with Tori and Lily, and working around the old house.

Maybe Eddie and Tori were right. He wasn't the same man who'd walked away from this life all those months ago. The idea of going undercover used to excite him and get his blood racing. His thoughts would be consumed with scenarios he could employ, the skills he would use, and he'd anticipate the huge adrenaline rush that accompanied the takedown.

But today he only felt dread and apprehension. He rarely thought about being killed on the job. All agents knew it was a possibility, but they locked it away in the dark corners of their minds and did their jobs. Now, Reid looked at the specter of death with new eyes. There'd been no one in his life to care if he lived or died. Now there were people who would miss him, grieve for him.

More important, he didn't want to be separated from them. He wanted time together, lots of time, years of time. Emotions were now his enemy, and the biggest threat to his going undercover. One stray thought could distract his focus, one misspoken word could blow his cover, one sweet second of a memory could cost him his life.

His boss droned on. The sound of his cell phone buzzing was a welcome interruption. He pulled it from his pocket. The name on the screen raised the hair on his neck. Hamilton Haven.

"You have something more important to do?"

Novak's tone clearly revealed his irritation.

There'd been a time when he would have ignored the call and kept his focus on the job ahead. He stared at the phone. He stood, tossing a glance over his shoulder at his boss. "I have to take this." He strode to the hall, a canyon of fear opening inside him.

"Mr. Blackthorn, this is Dr. Kennedy at the Hamilton Haven. I'm afraid your brother Edward's condition has taken a downturn. There's nothing we can do. I've called in hospice care, but I give him a day or two at most. I think you should come right away."

His chest constricted with pain. He'd known Eddie was running out of time and he'd tried to prepare himself, but now it was all too imminent. He wasn't ready to lose his brother. "I'll leave now."

Reid ran a hand through his hair, praying Eddie would hold on until he got there. But first he had to correct something. He stepped into his boss's office. "I'm not coming back. This was a mistake."

Novak yanked off his glasses and glared. "Blackthorn, you're the best we have. This assignment is tailor-made for you. You'd be a fool to turn this down. The only mistake you made was leaving in the first place. We need you on this job."

"No. Leaving this job was the best thing

I ever did. Sorry, Len. I'm not qualified for this line of work any longer. My family needs me more."

The main kitchen smelled like blueberry muffins and fresh coffee. Tori smiled and inhaled the sweet aroma. The Smiley girls' recipes had triumphed again. They were perfection. So far every one she'd tried had been better than the last. Her morning menu was complete. She'd found a special item for each day of the week, delicacies that would greet her guests each morning and start them on their way. Baking had kept her occupied since Reid had left, and had prevented her from missing him too much.

Lily skipped into the kitchen and climbed up on the stool. "Can I have one?"

"Sure, but be careful. They're hot."

"I think Mr. Reid would like these. Can we take him one?"

Lily was having a difficult time accepting that Reid had gone away, and Tori had struggled to explain the difference between her mother going away forever and Reid going away for a short while. Time held little meaning for a five-year-old.

Buster stretched out on the floor beside Lily's stool and growled low in his throat. Tori pulled apart a muffin, put it on a plate, then placed it in front of Lily. "The next time he comes to visit, I'll make these especially for him and you can help."

"Really? I want to cook like you do."

"And I'd love to teach you. It'll be fun baking things together."

Buster's growl grew deeper.

Lily glanced down at the dog. "Maybe Buster wants one, too."

The animal jumped up and barked.

"Is that a yes, fella?" Tori chuckled. "Sorry, no people food for you."

Buster trotted to the hall and barked again. What was wrong with that mutt?

She walked to the hall. Buster was looking at her. He barked several more times and ran toward the formal dining room. His bark became urgent, and Tori's concern spiked. She hurried to the room, but everything looked normal. Buster ran to the door at the far end that connected to the tearoom. His barks were frantic now.

She took hold of the doorknob. It was hot. Smoke crawled out under the door.

Fire. Her house was on fire.

After a mad dash back to the kitchen, she grabbed her phone and called the fire department as she scooped up Lily with her free arm and carried her outside, far from the house. Within minutes, the scream of sirens filled the air. The squeak and grind of large wheels told her the fire trucks had arrived. Someone else must have seen the fire before her and called it in.

She held Lily in her arms, hearing her soft sobs against her neck. "Shh. It's going to be all right. The firemen will put out the fire."

"I don't want our house to burn."

"I know. Don't worry. We can fix it."

"Will Mr. Reid come back to help?"

Tears stung her eyes. If only. She wished he was here to hold her and tell her everything would be all right.

"Tori, are you okay?"

Naomi Foster hurried into the yard, her features filled with concern. "I saw the smoke and called the fire department. I tried to call you, but it went to voice mail. I hoped you were safely away."

"We're fine. The dog alerted us to the smoke." Buster. Where was Buster? As if knowing she needed him, the dog trotted down the drive and into the yard. Tori scratched his head. "You're a hero again, fella. Thank you."

And to think she'd never wanted this mutt

in the first place. How many ways had Reid's appearance in her life changed things? Her gaze drifted to the roof, where she could see water spraying over the top and dark smoke curling into the trees and up toward the clear sky, taking all her hopes and dreams with it.

There would be no grand opening of Camellia Hall now. Or ever. The pain was so deep she couldn't even find tears for it.

It was all Reid could do to keep his vehicle at the speed limit. Houston was six hours from Dover, longer if the traffic was bad. What he wouldn't give for a pop-on red light and a siren. He settled for endless prayer and some serious soul-searching. Even so, the towns crawled by. Orange, Texas. Lake Charles, Louisiana. Lafayette.

Outside his windshield, the tops of trees peeked over the elevated Interstate 10 and stretched for eighteen miles. Below, the Atchafalaya Basin spread out for hundreds of miles. With the sky above and the water far below, the route always made him feel as if he were flying.

An incoming call appeared on the screen of his Bluetooth. Jim Fuller.

Jimmy Ray. Why would he be calling? A knot of concern formed in his gut.

"Hello."

"Reid?"

The tension in his friend's tone sent his stomach clenching. "Yeah. What's going on?"

"I wanted to let you know about the fire in case you hadn't heard."

"Fire?"

"Tori's house caught fire last night."

His blood iced. "Is she all right? Lily?" Visions of his girls trapped in smoke or flames stopped his heart.

"They're both fine. The fire was in the tearoom. The rest of the house is untouched, but it doesn't look like the B and B will open on time."

Reid's throat constricted at the thought of Tori's dream going up in smoke. He could only imagine her heartbreak. "Why didn't she call me?"

The connection went silent a long moment. "You left."

Yes. He'd left. He'd walked out because he was scared, and he wasn't sure he could measure up to the man Tori needed him to be. Truth was, he was afraid to let go of the old life, the old need for justice. It had been a part of him for so long he wasn't comfortable anywhere else. What was it Eddie had said about stepping out of his comfort zone being the only way to find happiness?

"I'm already on the road. And, Jimmy Ray, thanks."

"I thought this might clear things up in your head, seeing as how you've been all upside down and backward these last few days."

Jimmy Ray understood the struggle to leave a career in law enforcement and learn to live a life of peace and contentment. But Reid knew what he wanted now, and it was back in Dover, not in Lubbock. He only hoped it wasn't too late.

At Baton Rouge, Reid merged onto Interstate 12, his nerves on edge and his mind in turmoil. Dover was still an hour away.

Would Tori be glad to see him? Or would she be angry he'd left her and Lily when they'd needed him most? Once again, he'd failed those he loved. If he'd stayed like Tori had asked, he would have been there, and maybe he could have spotted the fire sooner.

Useless speculation. He'd have to admit his mistake, promise her he'd stay by her side forever, that he'd do whatever it took, whatever risks necessary to become the man she needed and, God willing, a father to Lily.

As the road stretched out ahead, Reid faced one of the hardest choices of his life. The I-55 interchange was ahead. If he merged onto I-55 North he would head toward Dover, where he could make sure Tori and Lily were all right. But if he took the exit ramp, it led him into Hammond and his brother, who was losing his battle and needed him now more than ever.

His heart was wrenched in two.

He took the exit to Hammond.

The smell of smoke and burnt wood stung her nostrils. Tori stood inside the doorway from the main house the next afternoon, taking in what was left of the tearoom. Blackened walls, charred remnants of tables and chairs, broken windows, the outside wall and most of the lower porch on that side were completely gone. The fire marshal speculated a faulty wire might have started the blaze, but he wouldn't know for sure until the inspection was done.

Thankfully, the insurance adjuster had assured her she was covered for all damages. But the time lost wasn't recoverable. Her grand opening was on hold. Indefinitely. Turning away, she fought the tears welling up behind her eyes. Her beautiful house was scarred, and she was in danger of never fulfilling her dream. She wanted to yell. She wanted a hug.

She wanted Reid. He always made her feel

stronger. He made her believe that no matter what happened, she could succeed. She especially appreciated that Reid believed she was the perfect mother for Lily.

She missed him. Lily had cried herself to sleep nearly every night he'd been gone. Tori had shed a few tears herself, but hers were more in worry for Reid and his safety for when he went back undercover. Mostly she missed having him close. Too late, she'd realized how much she loved him, and how deeply he was engrained into her life and her heart.

The opening notes of her favorite hymn made her reach for her phone. She inhaled sharply when she saw the name of the nursing home. Eddie. "Hello?"

"Is this Victoria Montgomery?"

"Yes. Is this about Eddie?"

"He left your number as a secondary name to notify in case of emergency. I'm afraid he's not doing well. His condition has deteriorated."

Tori bit her lip. "How bad is it?"

"A matter of days. All we can do now is make him comfortable."

"Thank you for letting me know."

Tori sank into the antique bench in the hallway, her mind weighed down with regret. She'd known Lily's father was dying. It was the reason Reid had tracked them down. But now that his death was around the corner, her mind-set was shattered. How was Reid taking the news? Should she call him? He must be hurting. She knew the pain of losing a loved one. Her father had died suddenly over two years ago, and she'd responded by running away to stay with Judy. Losing Judy had been another blow.

But despite the loss, her last moments with Judy had been tender. The day before her father died, they'd had lunch together and made plans for her next adventure. And what about Lily? She'd had a chance to say goodbye to her mother. Shouldn't she have the same chance with her father? She still believed Lily was too young to know the whole truth, but Reid was right. One day she would ask, and how would Tori respond when Lily learned she had a father, but had been kept from him by a request from a bitter woman?

What was the right thing to do? She'd made a promise to her friend. Loyalty was important, but she was Lily's mother now. Lily even called her that. So whose wishes did she honor?

She bowed her head, seeking guidance. *Please Lord. Show me what to do.* Like the sun suddenly appearing from behind the clouds, she realized what she'd been doing. Heat, hot and condemning, surged through her veins.

All this time she'd prayed for strength and wisdom to raise Lily. She'd prayed for help with the house and her new business. She'd prayed for Lily and her broken heart, for her to know she was loved. She'd prayed for a peaceful passing for Eddie and comfort for Reid when the time came.

But she'd never prayed for a solution to the conundrum she and Reid faced. Why? Because she had been afraid the Lord would tell her what to do, and it wouldn't be what she wanted to hear.

Once she agreed to a meeting with Eddie and set aside her promise to Judy, then she'd have to face the truth about a lot of things. Like her growing realization that she loved Reid Blackthorn. That her friend hadn't been as sound of mind as she'd believed, and that Lily might be happier knowing about her dad. And she'd have to admit that having Reid around the old home was something she wanted to continue—forever.

She began to fear her stubbornness, her dogged determination to keep her promise that had only widened the chasm between them. There'd been a point at which she thought they could have a relationship. But now it had gone on too long. Eddie was quickly reaching the end of his life. Reid would never forgive her if he died without ever seeing Lily.

There was only one thing to do.

The sun was setting when Reid arrived at the hospital. His heart was still torn between losing his brother and his need to return to Dover, but his prayer now was that Eddie would hold on long enough for him to say goodbye and ask his forgiveness again.

As he rounded the corner toward his brother's room, he noticed the mother and child walking ahead of him. He stopped, questioning his eyesight. "Tori?" The woman turned around. The smile on her face sent his pulse racing.

"Reid."

Lily squealed and raced toward him. "Uncle Reid! I missed you so much!" She launched herself into his arms, hugging his neck so tightly he found it hard to breathe.

She smiled and started placing little kisses on his cheeks. Tori came to his side, her gaze locking with his.

"What are you doing here?"

"I've brought Lily to see—your brother."

Reid frowned.

"I told Lily you're her uncle. She's very happy about that. I haven't told her anything else yet."

"How did you know about Eddie's condition?"

"They called me. Apparently Eddie gave them my number as a backup."

He looked her over and scanned Lily, still in his arms. "The fire. Are you both okay?"

"How did you find out?"

"Jimmy Ray. How bad was it?"

"We were lucky. The tearoom is gutted, and the porch is gone, but the rest of the house is fine."

He pulled her into his embrace, wanting to keep her there forever, safe from any harm. "I could have lost you both. I should have been there to protect you."

"That's not important now. We can talk about it later. What matters is Eddie." She laid her palm against his cheek. "I'm sorry it took me so long to do this. I thought I was honoring Judy's wishes, but I realized all I was doing was continuing her bitterness. I don't want that to be part of Lily's future."

Reid placed his hand over hers before lifting it and kissing her palm. "Thank you. Let's go see him together."

The room was silent, with only the soft

beeping of monitors disturbing the quiet. A nurse sat beside the bed. She looked up and nodded as they entered. "Mr. Blackthorn. I'm glad to see you. He's been asking about you. Is this your family?"

It would be, if he had anything to say about it. But there was no time for explanations. He made the introductions and she left them alone. Tori's fingers fluttered in his as they approached the bed. Was she as nervous as he was? Eddie seeing his daughter for the first time came with risks. Would his brother blurt out the truth? How would he react? He'd waited so long for this moment.

"Eddie. I've brought Lily to see you."

Slowly the dark eyes opened, and Reid's gut kicked at the deep pain he saw. He knew the medications being fed into Eddie's body would ease his physical pain, but it was his emotional pain he saw now.

"Lily?"

Reid swallowed the grief scratching his throat. "Yes." He sat in the chair and held his hand out to Lily. His next big concern was for her. Would she be scared seeing all the tubes and monitors? "Lily, this is my brother, Eddie."

She leaned in against Reid, studying the man in the bed. "Hi."

Eddie smiled, the darkness in his eyes coming to life again. "Hello. I'm very glad to meet you. Thank you for coming to see me. My brother has told me all about you."

Lily studied him a moment. "Are you sick like my mommy was?"

Reid heard Tori's soft gasp.

"Yes. I am."

"My mommy went to live with Jesus. Is that where you're going?"

Eddie held out his frail hand to her. "I'm certain of it."

Lily placed her little hand in his and smiled. "I hope you like it there."

"I know I will."

"Eddie, this is Tori Montgomery. The woman I told you about."

"The one you talk about all the time, you mean. She's much prettier than you let on, big brother."

Tori stepped forward. "I'm pleased to meet you, Eddie. I'm sorry it took me so long to agree to come."

"No need to explain." Eddie drew in a slow, ragged breath. "Judy had every right to hate me. The thing is, I loved her more than anyone, but I was a coward, too afraid to stay and learn to be a husband and father." He inhaled again. "I didn't think I could handle it.

So I walked way, and as a result she grew to despise me."

Tori laid a hand on his arm. "That's not completely true. I found her journal, and in it she talked about how much she loved you and how much your leaving hurt. I think her bitterness grew from there, but deep down she loved you, too."

Eddie moved his gaze to Lily, who had wandered to the small table near the window and was scribbling away on a piece of paper. "Thank you for bringing her. Please don't let her grow up hating me."

Tears blinded her. "I promise. And one day I'll tell her all about you. Reid and I both will."

Lily returned to the bedside, paper in her hand. "Uncle Reid's brother, will you give this to my mommy when you see her in Jesus' house?"

Eddie took the paper, his eyes closing briefly. "I'd be happy to."

Lily took Eddie's hand. "Tell her I love her and I miss her, but I love my new mommy, too."

"You are a sweet little girl, Lily. Just like your mother. Thank you for coming to see me."

Reid saw the fatigue overtaking his brother. His breathing was becoming more labored.

It was time to go. He patted Eddie's shoulder. "You need to rest. I'll be back to see you later today."

Eddie whispered, "No. Go home with your family. It's where you belong."

Reid joined Tori and Lily in the hall, his heart torn to shreds. Why had he waited so long to find his brother again? Why had he been so blind to what really mattered? Eddie was right. He belonged with Tori and Lily, but despite the attraction between them, there was a river of differences he wasn't sure they could overcome.

"I like your brother, Uncle Reid."

"He liked you, too, Lily, and he's very glad you visited him." Reid looked at Tori. "I'll follow you home. We need to talk about things."

Tori shook her head. "Not now. You need to be with Eddie. We can talk later. Floyd starts reconstruction tomorrow, and I need to be there."

Like taffy being pulled on a machine, Reid's emotions were twisted and folded into knots. He wanted to go home to Dover with Tori, but he needed to be here. "All right. I'll keep you updated on things."

"Take your time. We'll be there waiting when you come home."

Her words gave Reid hope. He grabbed it

with both hands and his whole heart. "Thank you for coming. I know how hard this must have been for you."

She smiled up at him, her blue eyes filled with delight. "Actually, it wasn't as hard as I'd expected because I was doing it for someone I love."

She stood on tiptoe, kissed his lips briefly, then took Lily's hand and walked away. He knew she had come because of her love for Lily. He was simply grateful that she'd made it in time for Eddie to see his little girl.

The weather was unusually warm and sunny for late November in Mississippi. Perfect porch-sitting weather, and Tori was taking advantage of it. She kept her gaze focused on the row of charming white rockers on the west end of the house, where a porch swing moved gently in the breeze. If she looked toward the other end and the ugly charred remains of the tearoom, she'd start to weep.

Reconstruction had been delayed due to insurance red tape, but Floyd assured her he would start work the moment everything was settled. With no deadline looming, Tori had nothing pressing on her mind except for Reid. Eddie had passed away two days ago, and Reid's brief phone call had left her concerned for his emotional state. He'd refused her offer to come down to the nursing home, since there would be no formal funeral per Eddie's request. He promised her he'd come back to Dover as soon as possible.

The sound of a familiar vehicle broke into her thoughts. Lightness flooded her chest and brought a smile to her face when she saw Reid's truck pull to a stop at the curb. As she watched him come up the front sidewalk, her heart warmed with love. Oh, how she'd missed him. He looked incredibly handsome in his faded jeans and the pale green crewneck sweater that even from this distance called attention to his soft brown eyes.

She met him halfway, wrapping him in a warm embrace. "I'm so sorry about Eddie."

He nodded silently, pulling her tighter against him. When he stepped back, his eyes were moist.

"He's okay now. No pain or regrets, but I miss him. How are you and Lily?"

"Fine. Missing you. Buster will be thrilled you're here. He's inside with Lily."

Reid scanned the fire damage, pulling her against his side. "I'm so glad you weren't hurt. I don't know what I would do if anything happened to you."

"Buster was the hero again. He alerted us to the smoke."

"He's turned out to be a pretty valuable mutt. When will Floyd start rebuilding?"

"Soon."

He nodded, then looked into her eyes. "Can we talk?"

"Sure." She took his hand and strolled through the yard toward the giant willow near the edge of the property. Its weeping branches resembled golden raindrops as they spilled toward the ground. She stopped at the small bench near the edge of the tree, close to an old camellia bush heavy with red blossoms in full bloom. She sat and pulled him down beside her.

"I'm glad you didn't go back to work with the DEA. What will you do now?"

He angled to face her. "You were right. I'm not the same as I was. I can't live that life anymore. Which brings me to this. I have a proposition for you."

"Don't you mean a proposal?"

"What?"

She smiled. "Never mind. Go on." She slipped her arm in his, relishing the closeness. Everything was right in her world now. Reid was home.

"I'd like to become a partner in the business. The money our parents left us has never been touched. It's a considerable sum. It would give you financial stability and enable you to open for business on a sound footing."

"Partnership. Is that all you're offering?"

Reid blinked. "Well, I won't interfere with any decisions you might make as far as the B and B is concerned. I'd be a silent partner only."

Tori stood, moving off a few steps, and crossed her arms over her chest, trying to hide her amusement. Was he really so clueless? "Nope. No deal." She shouldn't tease him like this, but it was fun to see her big strong agent flustered. She'd tell him later that Eddie had called the evening of her visit and told her Reid was in love with her but was too skittish to say anything. She'd have to take the initiative. Well, that's exactly she was doing.

"Tori, I don't think you understand. This would allow you to enjoy the bed-and-breakfast and never have to worry if the rooms were full or not."

She faced him, fighting to keep a smile from her face. "No. Out of the question. I'm not settling for halfway. I won't accept anything other than full ownership."

He rose and came toward her, his forehead creased. "I don't understand."

She smiled and stepped close, resting her hands on his chest. "I know you don't. Which is why I have a proposal for you. I'm offering joint ownership in Camellia Hall with me, but only on a permanent basis."

"Permanent?"

His gaze locked with hers, seeking an explanation. She'd teased him long enough. She touched his cheek. "Total commitment. With a ring and a marriage license and a wedding, and all the other things that go with a lifetime commitment."

Reid's dark eyes brightened, and the smile she loved spread across his face. "Are you asking me to marry you?"

"Us. Me and Lily. She loves you, too, you know."

"And I love her. And you." He tugged her close and kissed her thoroughly. A kiss that held a promise for tomorrow and all the days ahead.

He cradled her face in his hands. "I realized what I want is right here—keeping this old house together and taking care of you and Lily."

"I'm glad you finally came to your senses."

He kissed her temple. "When would you like this partnership to begin?"

"I was thinking early next week. At the courthouse. Just the three of us."

He laughed. "You don't waste any time, do you?"

"Not when I know what I want."

"Won't your family be disappointed we're not having a real wedding?"

She slipped her arm around his waist. "I've had three almost-real weddings of my own, and my brothers and sister have all gotten married in the last two years. They'll probably be glad to be spared yet another one."

He captured her gaze. "Are you sure? You don't need more time to think about this?"

"Do you?"

"No. I've been sure for a long time."

She slipped her hand in his. "I've never been more sure of anything in my life. I always felt these nagging doubts in my other relationships. I thought there was something wrong with me. But now I realize on some level I knew they weren't the right ones, because all that time I was waiting for you."

"Uncle Reid!"

Lily raced across the yard, Buster on her heels. She propelled herself into his arms and he held her tight, his heart filled with more love than he'd thought possible.

"Are you home for always now? 'Cause we don't like it when you're gone."

"Yes, I am. Forever this time."

She squealed and clapped her hands, then wiggled to be set down. She grabbed Buster and hugged his neck. "Buster is happy, too." She smiled up at him. "Want to see my new spinny dress?"

Reid looked at Tori. "Uh, sure."

"Watch." Lily spun around in a circle, causing the skirt on her purple dress to flare out in the air. "Isn't it beautiful?"

"It's perfect."

Tori slipped her arm around his waist as they started back toward the house, Lily and Buster playing happily on the lawn.

"I'm sorry you won't open in time for Thanksgiving like you planned."

"Me, too. But the Lady Banks Inn has graciously taken in my few guests at a reduced price. The house won't be open until spring at the earliest, but until then it'll simply be our home. We can use the time to enjoy being a family before we throw open the doors to others."

"As co-owner, I approve your plan. I want nothing more than to have my girls all to myself for a while."

"You never answered my question. Will you be a full partner in this business?"

"I accept your proposal."

Tori snuggled close to his side. With Reid and Lily as her family, she'd finally found her true purpose in life.

Epilogue

Camellia Hall had never looked more perfect.

Tori Blackthorn stood at the head of the long dining room table, her heart overflowing with gratitude and thankfulness.

The Thanksgiving table was set with a vintage lace tablecloth, upon which rested the blue-and-white china she'd selected from the patterns that had come with the house. Etched stemware glistened in the sunlight. Antique silverware shone against the delicate settings. Tiny rainbows danced around the room, refractions from the French crystal chandelier overhead.

Her gaze drifted to the end of the room and to the parlor across the hall, where the three-tiered wedding cake was displayed along with colorfully wrapped gifts.

Today, Thanksgiving, would also be a day

of celebration for her marriage to Reid three days ago. Her new husband stepped to her side, and she captured his gaze for a long moment before turning to face her family all seated at the long table. Lily stood on the dining chair, one arm holding on to her mother.

"Reid and I want to tell you how much it means to us to have you all here for our first Thanksgiving together in our home. I know this all happened suddenly, but I think we both knew from the beginning that we were meant to be together. It just took us a while to figure it out."

"But when you did, pow." Tori's brother Linc made a rocket gesture with his hand. "You didn't waste any time."

Her brother Gil raised his hand. "I'm glad I didn't have to wear another monkey suit."

The women all expressed their disapproval. Tori's sister, Bethany, sent a glare in the direction of her brothers. "Don't listen to those clowns. I think your courtship is the most romantic thing I've ever heard."

Seth leaned forward. "I think baby sister did okay. Reid, we're glad you're part of the family."

"Uncle Reid is my new daddy," Lily said. "Isn't he beautiful?"

Laughter rippled around the room.

"There's only one person missing. Dad. But I think he'd be happy to see how much our family has grown. I know he would love each and every one of our new family members. We have so much to be thankful for this year."

Tori picked up her glass. "My life is so full of blessings, it would take me a lifetime to list them all." She looked up at Reid, his eyes full of love, causing her pulse to jump. "Mostly, I'm thankful for this man, who has shown me I'm stronger than I thought, and that together we can accomplish anything we set out to do. I love you."

Reid kissed her soundly and held her close to his side. Lily giggled. The family cheered.

Tori blinked away tears and looked at the full life in front of her, overcome with happiness.

"Happy Thanksgiving, everyone."

* * * * *

If you loved this tale of sweet romance,
pick up these other stories
in the HOME TO DOVER *series*
from author Lorraine Beatty:

REKINDLED ROMANCE
RESTORING HIS HEART
PROTECTING THE WIDOW'S HEART
HIS SMALL-TOWN FAMILY
BACHELOR TO THE RESCUE
HER CHRISTMAS HERO
THE NANNY'S SECRET CHILD
A MOM FOR CHRISTMAS
THE LAWMAN'S SECRET SON

Dear Reader,

I hope you have enjoyed your ten-book journey to the small town of Dover, Mississippi. This is the last in that series and the final story for the five Montgomery siblings. Tori and Reid have both made promises they are determined to keep, and both have let their loved ones down in the past and are desperate to avoid repeating that mistake. Yet only one of them can keep their promise. Someone has to compromise.

We all make promises that we may not be able to keep. We all wish we could correct bad choices and ill-advised decisions. But we can't always go back and fix mistakes or take a different path. The only way to let go of the guilt and regret is to place them in the Lord's hands and move forward with love and trust. Reid and Tori learn that's not an easy thing to do. When someone has hurt us, it's hard to forgive and show compassion, but unless we do, unless we learn to compromise, the impasse will never be overcome.

I hope Reid and Tori's journey will give you new insight and encouragement into trusting and forgiving. We all struggle with these things daily.

I love to hear from readers. You can reach me through my website, lorrainebeatty.com. From there you can access my Facebook page and other social media links. Or you write to Love Inspired, 195 Broadway, New York, NY 10007.

God bless,
Lorraine Beatty